The Collection of THIRTEEN

The Collection of THIRTEEN

Callie Rae Sutton

Paperback publication 2023

Cover design by Amy Hunter
Edited by Mary E. Porter
Formatted by Kari Holloway

ISBN (paperback) 979-8-9885539-0-8
ISBN (ebook) 979-8-9885539-1-5

www.blushingcrow13.com

TABLE OF CONTENTS

Introduction

Triskaidekaphobia - the fear of the number thirteen. This fear has a long history of mythological superstition. For instance, in Norse mythology, twelve deities were invited to a banquet in Valhalla. My favorite trickster, Loki, who is considered to be the god of mischief, aka the trickster god, heard about the invitation, realized he wasn't among the chosen, and crashed the dinner party. At the event, another god, Balder, a favorite amongst the gods, perished, which they blamed on Loki, the thirteenth "guest".

Similarly, in Christianity, thirteen people sat down for the Last Supper—Jesus and twelve disciples, one of whom being the traitor, Judas. After Judas was paid his silver for his betrayal, Judas killed himself in despair of his contribution to Jesus' death.

The fear of 13 is so great in some countries that you can even hire someone to make your thirteen-guest dinner party go up to fourteen, just to avoid the number. Because Friday the thirteenth is especially looked down upon, some weddings, funerals, and other events are delayed just to avoid the day.

However, there are some who find the number, dare I say, lucky or just plain likable. For example, there was an opera composer, Richard Wagner (1813-1883), who loved the number. He composed thirteen operas and even disregarded his first name, Wilhelm, so that his name would be composed of thirteen letters. The United States' twenty-eighth president did the same to his name, choosing to use his middle name, Woodrow, rather than his first name, Thomas, thereby creating thirteen letters in Woodrow Wilson (1856-1924). This president often broadcasted important decisions on the thirteenth day of the month, showing no fear for this normally "fearsome" number.

There once was a group, created by William Fowler, that started on September 13th, 1881 and was comprised of twelve British journalists and a waiter who was invited to dine with them when the original thirteenth member did not show up. The name of this anti-superstitious group was called the "London Thirteen Club". Their mission was to reveal that the number wasn't as unlucky as everyone feared. Through the years, other chapters formed in New York, Chicago, France and even a group of thirteen women from Iowa. Even though they did everything possible to disprove the fear, such as meeting on the thirteenth and having thirteen people sit at the table, the fear of the two-digit number was too great. After Fowler died suddenly in 1897, the interest began to dwindle. By the 1920s, the only thing you'd see about the club in the papers were the obituaries of its former members.

I challenge you to pick up a one-dollar bill and count how many references of the number thirteen you see. Look at the "The Great Seal", which consists of the pyramid and the eagle's shield. The number thirteen is quite prevalent. There are thirteen levels in the pyramid, thirteen stars in the "Seal of the Department of Treasury", thirteen stars on top of the eagle, thirteen arrows in one of the eagle's talons, and thirteen leaves and olives in the branches held in the eagle's other talon. In this case, the number thirteen was to recognize the original thirteen colonies.[1]

---

1 Richard Webster, Encyclopedia of Superstitions (Woodbury, Minnesota: Llewellyn Publications, 2008), 253-255.

The number *thirteen* has always been a novelty to me. The fact that something as simple as a number could strike such intense fear into people is mind boggling. There are architects who design buildings and believe that taking said number off their elevator buttons will ease clients' minds. The even crazier concept is that it works!

Because of this, my favorite number happens to be lucky number thirteen, so I devised a collection based around the so-called taboo number—thirteen stories that revolve around the number thirteen. The genre ranges a great deal, including fantasy, crime, thriller, romance, adventure, drama, and coming of age.

Before you get to the stories themselves, I have included a couple sentences that give a short synopsis for each short story. I hope you enjoy them!

The Thirteenth Bell - This was the first story that I wrote for this collection. In all actuality, it inspired this collection. And oddly enough, it was the first story that I've ever written in which I came up with the title before the plot or characters.

I was getting ready for bed one night and I heard the nearby church's bell toll the hour. I thought, with my fascination with the number, *Wouldn't it be cool if there were a thirteenth chime and something magical would happen?* And so, I came up with the whole concept, characters, and wrote it within twenty-four hours of the initial spark.

When Melanie, a witch, is caught by the town's police chief, she has the opportunity to dive deep into her reasoning for the handful of people she has killed while she's interrogated. How did she get away with it for so long, and what is her cursed punishment?

The Thirteenth Number - Phobia: the extreme or irrational fear of something. The fear of the number thirteen has its own word, triskaidekaphobia. I didn't see it possible to write a collection revolving around the number without a story about the fear itself.

Corrin wakes up as she always does, but her day doesn't quite go to plan. Everything around her shouts the thing that she is most afraid of. Can she conquer it, or does it consume her entirely?

The Thirteenth Drink - I'm a lightweight, but I'm pretty sure that thirteen drinks is still quite a bit to keep down. I did a survey for this story, asking how "doubles" were counted. In conclusion, I have received a fairly unanimous vote that the bartender will count a double as two drinks, as this is how the price is figured. However, the majority of partakers count by the glass, making even a double, a single drink. Given these very loose statistics, I counted the drinks by the glass, from the perspective of the drinker.

A guy walks into a bar...sounds like a joke right? But when Roy drinks a few too many, his tongue gets a little too loose, and his bartender, Cody, gets an earful. Do the secrets stay within the confines of the bar, or will you read about it in tomorrow's headlines?

The Thirteenth Sacrifice - I know I tend to write some fairly dark twists and turns, but this one is by far the darkest that I have written. Cult life both terrifies me and peaks my interest at the same time.

You can't very well have a well-rounded collection without going from one extreme to the next, right?

What's the best way to get away with things? To be dead. At least that was the answer for Silas Grant. After almost being caught by the police, he sought "death" in order to continue his mission from a higher power. Will he get away with it again, or will someone best him even in his death?

The Thirteenth Candle - Coming-of-age stories are a pretty common trope, but that didn't stop me from creating this story. It is still interesting to me. The definition, age, and ceremony of this social concept varies a great deal in different cultures, and since I love a good witch story....

Allegra is finally thirteen, the age that any witch gets her primary magical powers and her familiar. When the familiars begin to talk, however, and the story behind the witch's gift in particular becomes apparent, that's when the magic truly begins.

The Thirteenth Angel - Oh my goodness, this story changed so many times before I decided on the ending concept. And even then, it continued to change as I wrote it. There are so many different references on angels. The one that showed up the most when I searched "the thirteenth angel" was *The Complete Books of Enoch: 1 Enoch: The Ethiopian Book of Enoch: The Book of Parables*.[1] In Chapter sixty-nine, there is a mentioned *Bezaliel,* known as the "Angel of Shadows". Bezaliel was the

---

1 Enoch (translated by R.H Charles and W.R. Morfill), The Complete Books of Enoch: 1 Enoch: The Ethiopian Book of Enoch: The Book of Parables (Wildian Press, 2021), 66-69.

thirteenth "watcher" of some twenty leaders of the two-hundred fallen angels.

Upon that discovery, the concept of the reaper came to mind and how his reputation is sometimes confused with that of the devil himself. So in this story, I wanted to show a side of a reaper that many don't appreciate.

Bezaliel's twin brother, Lucifer, had already fallen to become the ruler of the dead. But when Bezaliel followed his brother, he didn't feel quite as at home. He lacked a sense of purpose that he so desperately craved. The only way to find such a thing is to go out into the world. He finds a friend who points him in the right direction.

The Thirteenth Soul - I've had this concept in my head for quite some time. It sparked when I saw a ouija board on the boardwalk while I was visiting my dad. No one was using it. It was just sitting there, all alone. Creepy? Yes. A fantastic story prompt? Most definitely.

The sea witch, Cordelia, is fed up with the humans making her oceans their garbage dump. When she discovers an object in the sea, she uses it to her advantage in an attempt to free herself from the ocean floor and teach the humans a lesson. But when she mistakens a victim's will, does her plan backfire, or do they combine forces?

The Thirteenth Anniversary - I actually cried while writing this one. Not that that says much, as I am a true Pisces and my emotions run my life. We always see the grief when someone dies, but will we ever know the grief on the other side of the veil?

After her husband passes, Kaite writhes in the grief of her loss, especially since his death was so near to their anniversary. As she goes through his belongings and the attached memories, she finds his last gift to her. But was it her happy ending?

The Thirteenth Floor - I love...let me repeat...I love the show *Supernatural*. There was no way I was going to miss out on the opportunity to write about a demon.

There have been too many accidents with this company; some believe it is the curse of the thirteenth floor. But when Peter's friend, Aaron, becomes a victim to the insane, Peter does his best to fight against it. The question is...Does Peter know whom, or what he is messing with?

The Thirteenth Headstone - In my mind, I pulled concepts from the 1970s' and 1980s' childhood. Though I wasn't there, *Stranger Things* and then later *The Goonies* helped with the culture and adventure of this story.

The local cemetery has a great deal of secrets, but none of them seem to match up. When the parents go on a double date, five kids are determined to uncover the true story about the nameless headstone. Do they find the treasure they were looking for, or are they just ghost stories?

The Thirteenth Key - I am a sucker for puzzles, the active ones at least. Scavenger hunts have always been a favorite of mine. Mix that with the love of *Alice*

In Wonderland by Lewis Carroll, and I came up with a unique hunt for you to enjoy.

Brie, after recently inheriting her grandmother's house, receives a letter in the mail, the envelope of which holds a key. Who knows what she'll unlock?

The Thirteenth Year - I changed the story that was going to be here at least three times. But after plotting this one out, I knew it was the perfect story for this collection.

You've heard the story. Boy and girl run into each other on the sidewalk, exchange phone numbers, go on their first date, and live happily ever after. But when Bethany recognizes Winston from thirteen years ago, she has a different ending in mind for him.

The Thirteenth Seal - This one gets a little dark, but wanted to play with a serial killer who knows how to make his mark. I will be working on a novel based on Detective Kimberly Welsh's most unique case files. This is the first case.

Kimberly Welsh is the newly appointed detective to a serious ongoing case. Every month for the past year, on the thirteenth, a body shows up with nothing more than the mark of the serial killer— a wax seal. Detective Kimberly Welsh is determined to break the case, but will she be able to nab them before he kills again?

THE THIRTEENTH BELL

The room was small, and though you could smell the cheap coffee the chief was drinking, there was also the stench of drunkards and blood from previous interviews lingering in the air.

Chief of Police, Charlie Gott, gulped down some room temperature coffee, set the mug down, then sat himself in the chair across from the lady. "Miss, let's go through this one last time from the top." He checked to ensure the recorder was on. "Today is November twelfth. The first victim…."

"I wish you'd stop calling them that. All the people I have killed had it coming."

"I doubt any jury of your peers would group a 'cheating boyfriend' into the same category as the others that you so called 'provided justice' to."

The woman shrugged. She was deceptively quaint. Her mousy-brown hair was wrapped up into a neat low bun. Her clothes were on the verge of frumpy, and, as expected, her demeanor was shy. But now, she was an open book…as if she had been praying for someone to catch her and rid her of this…whatever it was.

"Well?"

She narrowly glared at the chief with a cut-throat smile. She placed her cuffed hands on the table and leaned forward to talk even closer to the recorder. "My name is Melanie Zander, your humble librarian of Brookburn, Maine, and I killed David Ross."

David Ross was THE guy…one that someone like shy little me could only dream of. He was tall, dark, and handsome. Enough nerd to have common ground with me, but enough jock to make him sexy and desirable.

We met at an end-of-the-year festival on campus. I was next in line at the taco truck and he was talking to his buddies and walking without paying attention. Of course, he ran into me, making his drink spill all over my dress. Instead of walking away and laughing like his friends did, he stopped and did his laughable best to pat me down with the napkins that he clumsily grabbed from the food truck's counter. In the midst of patting my breasts down, he looked directly into my eyes with his bright blues and we both busted out laughing.

"I'm so sorry," he said.

"No. Not at all. Really, this isn't the first and I'm sure it won't be the last."

"Even still. Would you allow me to buy you your meal?"

I blushed. My cheeks got so warm. But I thought, who does that? Only a nice person, right? So, I said, "Sure."

He bought my lunch and we picnicked on a nearby bench. That was our first date.

Our relationship grew quickly after that. The summer break was something I had only read about in romance novels. We had picnics by the lake almost daily. We played like children at the park. And he took me to some fancy restaurants. I even had to go shopping and find something more elaborate than what I had in my closet. David Ross treated me like a queen, something that I had never experienced in my mundane life.

Fall classes eventually started and, naturally, we both got busy. Sometimes we wouldn't see each other until the weekends. That was hard. Really hard. So hard, in fact, that I decided to surprise him one night at his dorm room. He had mentioned a study session with some of his classmates, but everyone's got to eat, right? So, I packed up our little picnic basket, ran up the stairs, tiptoed to his room and quietly opened the door with the key that he had given me.

The lights were off, but I heard sounds. Then it hit me. I turned on the light, and there he was butt-naked in his bed with this blonde cheerleader-type bimbo.

"I thought you were different."

"I did tell you I was unavailable tonight."

"Yes. You are right. You did. You told me you were studying. Tell me, David, what subject is this?"

The bimbo reached for her glasses and sat up, bringing the covers up with her to cover her naked body.

"Technically, Women's Studies. She is the professor."

"Your degree is in engineering. You aren't even taking that class."

"Sure does look like he is." The blonde smiled and reached down to his nether regions.

"You disgust me." And I stormed out.

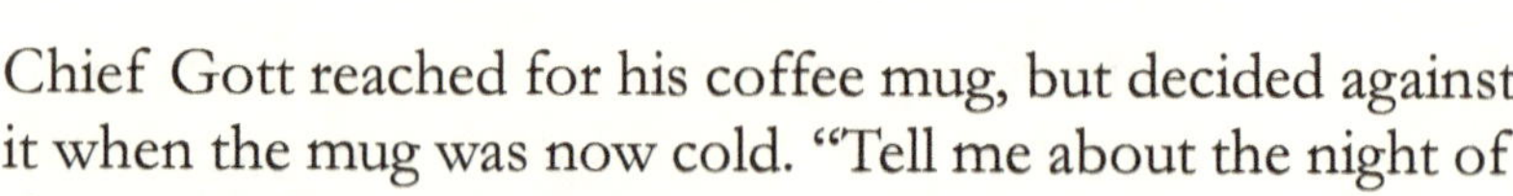

Chief Gott reached for his coffee mug, but decided against it when the mug was now cold. "Tell me about the night of the murder."

"Well, it was Halloween. Everyone was dressed up. David, like myself, loved the holiday, so I knew he was going to dress up. I figured he would go on the bar crawl like most of the college students did. I decided to dress up in a different costume than what I had originally picked out with him. This way, it would be easier for me to follow him. He was dressed as a pirate. I went with the Grim Reaper."

The chief scoffed. "Isn't that ironic."

"Glad you can appreciate it." She gave a curt smile, then said, "May I continue?"

"Please do."

We went from one bar to the next. He had no clue that I was even there. None. Which was great. To be honest, I don't really know why I chose to follow him. But I did. There was a chill in the air and the wind picked up. The moon was out. I don't know, maybe that's what got to me.

Anyway, he went down an alley by himself to take a piss. I stayed in the shadows against the wall. I could hear bells. One, two, three, four…. I got a little closer. Five, six, seven, eight, nine…. There was a pipe that I almost tripped on. The bell struck ten, eleven, twelve…. I reared back and swung with all my might. I swear I heard one more chime, then I honestly felt like I was soaring. I kind of blacked out a bit. I woke up the next morning in the bell tower of our fine town, Brookburn, with all the pirate's jewelry from David's costume, his dad's class ring his dad had given him before going to college, and his keys. I went home, saw his death on the news, and didn't look back.

Chief Gott stood up and grabbed his coffee. "No, you certainly did not. But you sure did look forward. Your next victim...."

"Rapist," Melanie corrected.

"We'll talk about that after I refresh my coffee. Would you like a water?"

"Please."

Melanie looked out the window. It was a bit blustery as she could see the trees sway and leaves form mini tornados. It was late afternoon, and she was surprisingly calm.

The chief came back in with a bag of chips for himself, his coffee, and a water. He handed the water to Melanie.

"Thank you."

He nodded his head. "Adam Mitt."

Melanie screwed the cap of the bottle back onto the bottle, swallowed, and scooted back into her chair.

Adam Mitt. What a shit-for-brains little boy in an adult body. My roommate, Abby, and I were getting ready for our dorm's Halloween party, which was actually the day before the holiday, as Halloween was on a Monday. That year we dressed together as sexy fairies, which was a bit out of my comfort zone, but I wasn't alone at least. We heard a knock at the door, and she answered it. I couldn't hear much, other than some mumbling, and then Abby shouting "No!" Then the door slammed.

When I asked her about it, she just said that this guy had been asking her out and she kept telling him no. We went about getting ready and headed downstairs to the common room. We danced all night and drank a lot. Abby and I went our separate ways at some point during the chaos. I woke up in our room, but I was just kind of sitting there in bed when Abby came in. She almost looked like a zombie.

"Are you alright?" I asked her.

She didn't answer. She took another step, but then she collapsed.

I turned on the light and went to her. Her lip was busted, one of her eyes was puffy and black, and her bottoms were all in disarray. I cried as I felt I already knew what had happened. I got her some water, draped a blanket over her, and carried her to the clinic. Abby, my best friend, had been raped. She refused to talk to the authorities or the medical personnel.

When she was released later that day, I took her back to our room. I propped her up in her bed, put on a show for her while I made some soup. When I brought her the soup, she grabbed it, reached for the remote and turned off theT.V.

"I don't want to make a big deal about this, but…" She started to tear up. "I have to tell someone. Can I trust you not to tell anyone?"

"You can count on me."

She nodded. "The guy who came to the door last night was Adam Mitt. He has grabbed me in the past and tried to steal a kiss. I slapped him. He came last night to attempt an apology but got too close and decided to grab my wrist as

I started moving away from him." She wiped her tears, but continued, "After you and I separated last night, he found me. I was wary, but he got me a drink and we talked. I remember getting tired, like, really tired. I woke up this morning, in his bed. He was in the bathroom. My head was pounding. Adam came out and said, 'I hope you enjoyed last night as much as I did. I told you I'd have you.' I started getting choked up. He said, 'Oh, are you going to cry now? You bitches are all the same, thinking you are here for more reasons other than to please the working man. Please.' I shook with fear, hate, and sadness. I leaped up to hit him, but he got to me first. He just kept going. Then stopped and said, 'I have to go to class now. Don't even think about telling anyone. You know they won't believe you anyway.' That's when I came back to the room."

My heart sank for her. No one asks for something like that, let alone deserves it. I knew what had to be done. I stayed with her until she fell asleep, grabbed a knife, then went out. I started to hear the bells again as I reached his dorm room. But this time, I had a feeling of empowerment, and I embraced it. It was raw but oddly justified. I knocked on his door and he opened it. Adam turned on his charm and tried grabbing me by the waist and said, "One fairy last night, and another tonight." On the tenth bell chime, I thrust the knife into his gut. I smiled as I heard the thirteenth bell and noticed I was flying. I went over his head as he fell to the ground, and flew out the window.

I was soaring in the sky with the stars and clouds. It was thrilling. I found myself going to the church bell tower. I looked at my reflection in the bell and saw myself as a crow. I went back to the body, as no one had found it yet, and I found myself attracted to his watch, his 'douchey' diamond earring, and a gold chain around his neck. I brought them back to the bell tower and stayed to admire my collection until the sun peeked through, and I noticed my talons turning back to feet. Soon, the reflection in the bell was little old me, Melanie Zander, and no longer the vigilante 'Crow', as you all so appropriately named me.

"A pretty realistic name given how I finally caught you, but we'll get to that. We have one more victim…my bad…one more 'villain' to discuss before we get to your most recent endeavors."

"Ah, yes. Julie Price. You guys dropped the ball on that one for sure."

"Hard to put together a case when no one has found the body."

"Maybe so, but I'm sure she would have cracked had you kept on her. You could tell from her baby shower that you and I both attended, as you may recall, that she was already having some trouble during the pregnancy."

"I didn't really notice anything."

"Go figure."

"Enlighten me then."

"That I will."

Julie had asked me to help her put together a book list for the baby, and I was all too happy to oblige as my new position at the library made me feel at home. I gathered some of the classics and some new ones and put them into a lovely basket, then showed up at the baby shower. Lots of people were already there, but I couldn't find Julie at all.

I took it upon myself to look around the house when I heard crying from the upstairs bathroom. I knocked on the door and Julie answered, "Just a minute." There was some shuffling of stuff, then the door unlocked, and there she was. Her eye make-up was leaking down her face and her eyes were a bit bloodshot from crying. When I asked her if she was alright, she just broke down again. I guided her back into the bathroom and asked what the problem was. She said something along the lines of, "I'm not ready to be a mother. What if I am horrible at it? What if this was a mistake?"

Knowing that she and James had been trying for years, I figured it was just the hormones. Not that I'm a mom and would know, but since I am adopted, I'm sure my birth mother had her reasons for giving me up.

Anyway, I did my best to reassure her that everything would sort itself out. She left the bathroom to join the party and I stayed to go to the bathroom, or at least, that's what I told Julie. In reality, I snooped. And what did I find, but none other than the duo "abortion pill" a.k.a mifepristone and misoprostol. Granted, as far along as she was, I'm not sure how effective it would have been, but I am sure it would have caused problems, regardless.

After that day, I kept my eye on her, just to be on the safe side. And I didn't see any other red flags until after the baby was born. She came into the library a few months after giving birth on a Saturday. I asked her how the baby was doing, but she seemed to be in her own zone and walked right past me. Soon, she brought up some books on post-partum depression.

I truly felt bad for her. I know James was a hard-working man; therefore, he normally left Julie at home alone with the baby all that time. But now, knowing her mental status, it worried me even more. I asked her if there was anything I could do, but still, no answer. I finished helping her check out, and she left. After that night, I made it a point to check on her every night. And every night, I saw James, Julie, and the baby, usually in James' arms, at the table having a nice family meal.

One night, I stopped by the house a little later than normal, as I had to reorganize the backstock shelving at work. I noticed the light in their bedroom turn off, so I assumed they had gone to sleep. But then, I saw a light come on in the baby's room. It was Julie. She was holding the baby in her arms, rocking back and forth. She leaned over and put the baby into the crib then turned to leave the room. I guess the baby started crying though because Julie turned back around. This time, she grabbed a pillow from the rocking chair and held it over the baby's face. I went into shock. I felt like I couldn't move. I should have knocked on the door and prayed she'd stop in time. But then I saw her remove the pillow and pick the baby back up, rocking it back and forth, making me believe that she hadn't gone through with it.

At some point, I made it back to my apartment, but I couldn't tell you how I got there. The next morning, I saw Julie on the news, stating that she went for her morning walk with the baby, turned around for a moment to get something out of her purse, and the baby was gone.

"I still don't understand why you didn't come to the cops about what you saw."

"Chief, knowing what you know now, about me, and my crow-like self, would you have believed me?"

"I don't know. But it would have given us more to go on. More of a focus."

"Chief, I wasn't a hundred percent sure that what I saw was what I saw. For all I know, she put the pillow in the crib with the baby, then picked it back up and continued to rock it to sleep."

"If you were in doubt, then why did you kill her?"

"I saw her with the body of the baby after the news report."

It was still bright on Halloween, but given the night's reputation over the past few years, thanks to yours truly, there was a curfew for trick-or-treating. Kids were all dressed up, giggling and running about. The crinkle of candy wrappers could be heard, usually followed by the parents saying, "Not yet."

I decided to take this year and not go on any wild adventures "i.e. not murder anyone" as I wanted to enjoy my few hours as a crow. Still human, I wandered the streets as the kids went up to strangers' doors and asked for candy. Then I saw Julie with a bundle of clothing behind her house while James was passing out candy on their porch. Remember, this was a month or so after the baby went "missing". I found my way to her and followed, again staying in the safety net of the shadows. She went down a few blocks and into the woods where the town witch, Narissa Cloud, lives.

She walked down to the creek back there and threw the bundle of clothes into the stream, then ran back into town. I followed the bundle, but it was in the middle of the river and it was going too fast for me to catch up. Before I lost sight, I saw a little hand unravel from the bundle.

I ran back to town as fast as I could. The town had fallen asleep early—again, you're welcome. I went to Julie's house and let myself in through the window; it was cracked open just enough. It was surprisingly nice weather for it to be the end of October. James was in his room, but Julie had been sleeping in the nursery. I picked up the same pillow that I had seen her with that night with her baby and held it over her face. She was shocked to see me sitting on her, rightfully so, I suppose, but you know the saying, "Karma's a bitch." You'd think she'd expected something to happen. Then I heard them. The bells. Like music to my ears. She stopped flailing, and on the thirteenth chime, I was my crow-self again.

"And that's when you took her wedding band, a silver baby rattle, and her locket with the picture of the baby inside."

Melanie nodded her head. "Once again, justice was served."

"Hum," the chief grunted. "Finally, we come to…"

"Mr. Kent Court. The perfect husband to Mrs. Natalie Court, who just happens to be one of my coworkers and friends. This one is easy enough. Kent was a highly sought-after lawyer, but he was fired a few months ago when the company noticed he was keeping two financial books. He was blackmailing his wealthy clients to pay him more to ensure a "not guilty" charge even though any jury could tell that his clients were dirty. That alone would qualify for my services if you ask me, but he took it further. A man with that big of an ego who was knocked down to nothing decided to pick up a new hobby of drinking and hitting Nat. A few weeks ago, she came into work with a busted tooth and some ribs that I was sure were broken. I knew exactly what to do. Trick-or-Treating was observed the day before this year."

"Gee. Can't imagine why."

Melanie rolled her eyes with a cockeyed smile. "No clue. Anyway, I was walking home from the library on Halloween and saw Mr. and Mrs. Court at the new Italian restaurant across the intersection from the library. I strolled by and saw their 'hushed' conversation was pretty intense. That meant tonight was the night, with my perfect alibi and all."

"Or so you thought." The chief had a big 'ol grin plastered on his face.

"Yeah, yeah. We get it—you caught me. Can I finish my story?"

He gestured with his hand for Melanie to proceed.

"I grabbed a hoodie and my gun from my car then waited for them to leave the restaurant. I ran over before they got to their car and grabbed her purse. Even though Mr. Court was an asshole, I knew the hero in him would help a damsel in distress and follow me to the alley."

"That is when Mrs. Court came back into the restaurant where she had remembered seeing me and my wife. I followed her out, but by the time I got to the alley, all I saw was Mr. Court on the ground, a bullet through one eye and claw marks on the other. Then, out of the corner of my eye, I saw a crow with shiny little knick-knacks in its beak and a talon."

"Some of my best work if you ask me. I took his cufflinks, watch, and the wedding ring that he didn't deserve. I didn't see you until dawn. I had decided to stay in my bell tower that night. When I turned back to human, you cuffed me and took me in. Congratulations, Chief Gott. You must be proud of yourself for such a win. A serial killer had been on the loose for too long."

"You came in so easily. Makes me wonder if you wanted to be caught."

Before Melanie could answer, there was a knock on the interrogation room door. Clerk Gavin Thorne came in. "Sorry for the interruption, but there is someone here who says they have some insight into the case."

"Who is it?"

"Narissa Cloud."

"I'll be out in a moment."

The clerk closed the door.

"I'll be right back."

"I'll be right here. Hey, you have the time?"

"Why, you have an important date? Am I keeping you?"

"Just curious." She shrugged her shoulders.

Chief Gott chuckled but checked his watch nonetheless. "Looks like we have been talking for a while. It is 11:45 pm. By the time I come back in, I'll have to restate the date on the recorder to November, Friday the Thirteenth."

"Wow, time flies when you're having fun. Before you leave, it is getting a bit stuffy in here, do you mind opening the window?"

He raised an eyebrow.

"Halloween is over and you have me cuffed. You really think I can leave?"

"I suppose not. It does get rather stagnant in this building." He opened the window just a crack and left.

Mrs. Narissa Cloud was waiting in the chief's office. She had long white hair, emerald eyes, and a soothing voice. She certainly fit the "town witch" description, but she was actually quite a nice lady and had been a part of Brookburn for quite some time.

"Mrs. Cloud. How can I help you?" The chief sat in his chair and Narissa Cloud began to speak.

"More like how I can help you. You see, my family goes back generations in this town. So far back that we were the starting point of the infamous witch trials. It was said long ago that our daughters would be cursed with a tormented life, and on top of that, the mother that would bring the child to witching age would then die soon after."

"That is quite a tale, but how is that helping me with the Melanie Zander case?"

"Chief." Mrs. Cloud shifted in her seat. "I am Ms. Zander's biological mother."

The chief all but fell out of his chair.

"You see, I fell in love, something that our bloodline was warned against as it usually leads to babies. You see our bloodline had also continued, despite such a curse, because there were no girls born. I was the first daughter in the family for generations. Most everyone had been lucky enough to have a son. My mother, unfortunately, wasn't so lucky. She passed when I was eighteen, the witching age in our family. Eventually, I fell in love. And I fell hard…too hard based on what my mom had warned me about. The love blinded me. We got married and got pregnant soon after. When we found out it was a girl, I panicked. I told my husband that the best point of action was to try something new. I suggested adoption. That way, I could skirt the curse's bylaws of raising a daughter to the witching age in hopes of saving myself from an early death and the torment destined to my daughter.

Chief Gott's jaw dropped so far it looked as though it might fall to the floor.

"My husband agreed. The Zander family picked her up from the hospital, and a week later, my beloved died. My loophole had cost me to lose the love of my life. However,

I was able to watch my Melanie grow into this beautiful young woman with a caring soul.

"On her eighteenth birthday, I stopped by the bell tower and waited for the thirteenth bell to toll, signaling her first transformation. Sure enough, she showed up. A flapping frenzy of feathers. The process takes a few years to get a hold of. As much as it was a joy to hold her and care for her, I cried, as my plan hadn't saved her from a life of torment. It only prolonged my life to watch everything unravel before me."

"Did you know the killings were from her?"

"Not at first, no. The first two were outside of town at the college. Part of me thought that if she left, it would do her well. To be away from the bell tower, you know? But when she came back, and the killings continued, I suspected. Then I saw her behind my house following that Julie woman, only to hear of her death the next day."

"You said on her birthday, she changed? I thought it was only Halloween."

Mrs. Cloud gazed down at the floor. One, two, three, four… The church bells echoed through town.

"Mrs. Cloud?"

Five, six, seven…

Narissa peered up and cracked the slyest of smiles. "Chief Gott. We can change only a few times a year: Halloween, our birthday…"

Eight, nine, ten, eleven.

"And Friday the thirteenth."

Twelve.

"Don't you move." The chief sprung out of the chair practically leaping over the desk, down the hall and opened the interrogation room door.

"Thirteen chimes, you've run out of time." Melanie cackled and shrunk into a magnificent crow.

The chief attempted to get to the window before her but to no avail. She squeezed right through the crack.

He ran back to his office to find his window wide open and papers flying everywhere. He ran out the building and looked up at the moon, shining bright with the silhouettes of two crows flying over the town's horizon.

THE THIRTEENTH NUMBER

A deep sigh escaped Corrin as she rolled over to take a peek at her alarm clock that had already gone off a few minutes prior. 6:12 a.m. Corrin quickly closed her eyes, rolled over, and covered her face with her blanket. She began counting to one hundred twenty, skipping, of course, the "evil" number to ensure that her day wouldn't start on the unfortunate thirteenth minute of the hour, but rather at 6:14 a.m.

"...119, 120." Corrin slowly turned back over. While taking in a shaky breath, she pried one eye open. "Good. Time to get up. I should not have slept in. I still have to make my bus. And, hopefully, I can get some coffee and a muffin."

After getting dressed and slapping on some makeup, she ran out the door with her briefcase. As she skipped down her steps, she noticed the seven in her address had fallen. Her heartbeat sped up and she broke out into an instant sweat. Corrin turned around to see 'one space three'. "Thirteen?" She picked up her seven to see if she could hang it back up. "Fuck." The nail was missing. "Well, I can't just leave it like that. What if I…" She used the metal seven to knock off the one and the three. "I can put them back up later, but at least my house won't be vibing with that number all day." She looked at her watch. "Shit. I've got to go."

In her peekaboo high heels, she ran down the street to the bus stop. "Just in time." The bus was in view, but as it got closer, she felt stuck in her spot with a sense of foreboding washing over her. "What is it with this blasted number today?"

The bus stopped, the driver opened the door. The other few people who were waiting boarded the bus. "Will you be joining us, Miss?"

"Where is bus five?"

"It broke down this morning. I was called to fill in."

Corrin forced a gulp, but still couldn't make herself move. The number thirteen kept flashing on the bus.

"Look, lady, I can't stay here forever. You either get on or watch me leave."

She looked at her watch again. If she didn't get on that bus, she'd most definitely be late. "I'm coming." She closed her eyes, held her breath, reached out her hand for the railing, and got on the bus.

The driver closed the doors and began to move before Corrin had a chance to find a seat. She opened her eyes and looked around. Twelve other people on the bus, eleven passengers and the bus driver. Now that she was on the bus, she made thirteen passengers. Thankfully, the bus driver stopped and reopened the doors to let on a straggler. She forced a breath and a smile and found a seat.

After a few minutes of collecting her thoughts, Corrin glanced out the window, and noticed that not only was the bus different, but so was the route. She could hear the blinker as the bus slowed down at the Main St. and 13th St. intersection.

Without hesitation, Corrin yelled, "Stop the bus." She scrambled to the front of the bus as the bus driver slammed on the breaks thinking that there was an emergency of some sort. "Let me out."

"Seriously? That isn't how this works. Go sit down and wait for the stop."

"Let. Me. Out." Corrin had tears sitting in her eyes. Her jaw was so clenched that the bus driver could see her jawline rhythmically change from soft to rigid.

The bus driver rolled his eyes, and not wanting to delay his route any further, he opened the door and let her out.

Knowing where she was, she back-tracked a block. Her office building was just a few blocks down, but she could take 12th St. instead. Looking at her watch again, the route had actually been faster than normal. "Good, I can stop and get breakfast and a coffee, which I desperately need."

Corrin walked down a little alleyway off of 12th St. that she thought would take her to the coffee shop next to her work. She had used it before, but this time, something felt off. It was broad daylight in spring, and yet the alley seemed cool and dark. Corrin felt a chilled drop of water on her skin. She looked up to see a dark cloud over her. She realized she had been walking a long time...longer than she should have to. She checked her watch, but it had stopped. Nearing panic mode, she looked up.

Finally, the coffee shop, "Sit and Sip" came into view, and her watch had started ticking again. She took a deep, calming breath. "Good, I've still got time."

She went right up to the counter as no one was in line.

"Welcome to 'Sit and Sip'. What can I get you?"

"A large coffee with cream and a blueberry muffin, please."

"We are actually out of muffins. Is there something else you'd like?"

"Um…" Corrin cringed her neck slightly to view her options on the menu listed above her. "How about a chocolate croissant?"

"Alright." The young lady entered the order into her register. "That'll be thirteen dollars and thirteen cents."

Corrin stepped back. Her breathing quickened and her face went pale. "Thirteen, thirteen…two thirteens." She mumbled. Lunging forward, she placed her hands on the counter and looked the lady dead in the eyes. "That can't be right. I normally pay seven fifty. I know I got a large coffee instead of the small, but that seems like a big increase."

"You also got a croissant, which is a bit more than our muffin. Our prices changed this week too. The total is $13.13."

Corrin unbuttoned the top button to her blouse to try to get more air. She could feel sweat dripping down her breasts. She backed up, stumbled over a chair and ran into the door, causing herself to trip on the threshold of the shop and fall onto the sidewalk.

"What is going on?" Corrin yelled out loud enough for people to turn and stare. Gazing up at the sky, still lying on the ground from her fall, she breathed in and out a couple times. *Seriously?! What is going on with this fucking number today?*

She stood up and reassured the small crowd that had gathered. "I'm fine. Really. Thanks." As the people dispersed, Corrin dusted herself off, buttoned up her shirt, and checked her watch once more. "What?" It was 7:26. "Where did the time go? And I didn't even get a coffee."

She kicked off her heels and ran in the direction of her building. "I made it!" After pushing open the glass doors, she slipped her shoes back on and swiftly walked towards the elevator.

"Miss Lewis…Corrin. Before you head up, your boss asked me to give you this note." The desk clerk handed Corrin a piece of paper that read:

Corrin,

>*Our dreams of expanding the business have finally come true. We now have two floors in this building to help with our increased clientele. The partners and I have agreed to promote you to the managing position on our new floor. Please report to your new window office on the thirteenth floor.*

>*Congratulations,*
>*Mr. Seamore*

"This can't fucking be happening. I can't do this." Corrin dropped her briefcase due to her shakiness. She could feel the blood drain from her face and her body warm all at the same time.

"Ma'am. Are you alright?"

"No. I don't believe so."

"Shall I call for someone? Mr. Seamore, maybe?"

"No. I just…I think I need some air."

Corrin pivoted on her heel, which broke, but it didn't seem to phase her as she clip-clopped out the building, onto the sidewalk, then out to the street.

"Ma'am!" someone shouted.

The whaling of an ambulance siren sparked Corrin out of her catatonic walk. Unfortunately, it was too late. The ambulance from station thirteen, ran right into her.

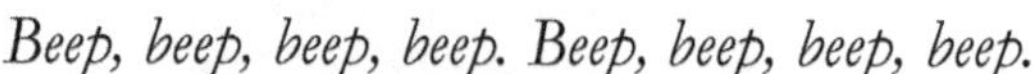

Beep, beep, beep, beep. Beep, beep, beep, beep.

"Ahh!" Corrin sprung up in bed. She reached over to shut off her alarm. 6:12 a.m. "What a fucking nightmare that was." …Or was it?

The Thirteenth Drink

It was damp out, but not raining anymore. The streets were pretty quiet, but given the hour, it made sense. Roy fluffed his trench coat collar up and ensured his coat was closed by patting down the front of his body. He secured his flat cap upon his head and opened the sturdy wooden doors.

There was an empty seat at the bar over in the corner where he had hoped he wouldn't be bothered. Keeping his coat on, he sat down and began tapping the counter, waiting for the bartender.

"Welcome to 'Nightcap Confessions', my name is Cody, and I'll be your bartender for the evening. What can I get you?"

"I need a 'Three Wise Men', please…and keep them coming." Roy slid a one-hundred dollar bill to him.

Cody nodded. "Coming right up."

Roy continued tapping the counter, watching as Cody grabbed a shot glass, Johnnie Walker Scotch, Jack Daniels, and some Jim Beam.

As soon as Cody placed the drink on the counter, Roy picked it up and slammed it down. "Another. In fact, how about you make this one a double?"

"Can do." Cody made the drink again, but given how quickly the first one disappeared, he didn't bother putting the bottles away this time. He looked over at Roy, who was still tapping the counter top and staring intensely at his soon-to-be refill. "Can I get you any food? The kitchen will close soon."

"No. I'll be drinking my dinner tonight."

"Want to talk about it? I'm pretty slow at the moment. It is a Tuesday, so I don't see it getting crazy in here or any-thing."

Roy looked around the room. He was right. There were a few couples in the table-sitting section, a couple on the other side of the bar, and a few single men spread out in the middle, one of whom was getting ready to leave.

"No. I'll just drink."

"Ok. Here you go." Cody placed the drink on the counter, and again, Roy quaffed the drink. "I'll get you an-other?"

Roy lightly pushed the glass towards Cody.

This time Cody was determined to be able to walk away for a moment. He made two doubles and placed them in front of Roy.

"You learn fast. Go ahead and help the others. I'll leave you alone for a bit."

Cody, proud of himself for being such an expert bar-tender, cracked a small smile and nodded to Roy.

Roy brought one glass up to his lips, took a sip, then put the glass down without letting go. He inhaled sharply, trying to control his breathing, then slowly blew the air out of his pursed lips. He finished the first drink in one chug, then reached for the second glass.

Swirling his glass around, Roy watched as the bar lighting reflected off the dark amber hue of the drink. His eyes began to sting as his focus was so intent, making his eyes water a bit. He cleared his throat and lifted his glass to his nose. The smell made him tear up even more, but that didn't stop him from drinking it as fast as he had before.

Though Roy was looking down at his two empty glasses, he could see Cody walking towards him. He let go of the glass, then gave a slightly less-tense smile.

"Another?"

"Please. Thanks. You know, I'm up for promotion?"

"Well, that seems to be something to celebrate. How about this one's on me? I can only do a single though, that okay?"

"I don't think a single will kill me." Roy chuckled. "Thank you."

Cody handed him the glass directly. "Cheers."

Once in hand, Roy elevated his glass to reciprocate "cheers". Another one down the hatch.

"I'll get you another?"

"Can I get two more doubles again?"

"Hmm. I guess given the circumstances, I can sneak you a couple more doubles, but then I'll have to bring you back to singles if you don't want any food…bar policy."

"Of course. That's fine."

Cody started pouring. "You sure you don't want any food?"

"Nah. I'm good."

"So, your promotion…?"

"Yes. I've been working towards making partner at 'Ellis and Grey Law Firm' for a few years now."

"Wow. That is quite an achievement."

"Yeah, I think so. It is very competitive. It's funny, I actually originally thought I was the only one up for it, but a few weeks ago, a bit of an underdog was thrown into the hat."

"Oh?" Cody brought the two drinks over to Roy, who didn't even let one touch the counter before he threw it back.

Roy sniffed in and took off his hat. His hair was black and you could tell that earlier in the day it had probably been slicked back. But now, it looked a bit disheveled and his brow was glistening with a thin sheen of sweat.

Roy opened his mouth to continue his story when the two men in the middle of the bar flagged Cody over to close out their tabs.

Roy nodded with a smile and motioned for him to help them. The couple on the other side of the bar were all that was left in the room. There was one family left in the sitting room, but they had been there for a while, so chances were they were getting ready to leave as well.

The men walked out of the bar. Cody double checked on the couple, who seemed to be in need of a room. There was more groping than drinking going on.

Roy sipped down his seventh glass then stood up. "Going to hit the head. I'll be back." He pushed his seat back and stood with a minimal amount of swaying.

Cody grabbed the two empty glasses from the counter and put them in the sink. He mixed another drink, this time a single and placed it in the empty spot where Roy had been sitting. A shiny glimmer of red caught Cody's attention. A small circle of what looked like blood sat on the backed-up stool. Cody came out from behind the bar to wipe it clean and noticed some scuffed blood on the floor as well, leading to the bathroom.

Cody ran to the bathroom door and knocked. "Sir, are you okay in there? I've noticed some blood on the floor and stool."

"Oh. Yeah. I'm alright. I had a nosebleed earlier. I must have missed some spots. I apologize for the trouble."

"No. No trouble. Just making sure you're good."

"I am. I'll be out in a moment."

Cody wiped up the remainder of the blood and checked on the couple again, who was ordering another round for themselves. By the time Cody turned back around, Roy had already come back from the bathroom, and chugged back the drink that was left for him.

Cody walked over to Roy, who, though still wearing his trench coat, looked sloppy. His buttons weren't in line, his collar was now down and slightly twisted, and there were visible sweat marks around his arm pits.

"Wanna call it a night, sir?" Cody suggested.

"Nah. Just getting started. I'm celebrating, remember? Plus, I haven't finished telling you my story."

Cody let out a short sigh and shrugged his shoulders. "I'll get you one more. But how about I call you a cab?"

"No. I'll hang out here for a while longer."

Cody shook his head but mixed another "Three Wise Men".

"You guys sure do like it hot in here. Or is that just me?" Roy burst out a laugh, fumbled to take his coat off by turning in circles, like a cat chasing its tail, then threw it on the floor.

Cody glanced up with Roy's drink in hand, but he almost dropped it when he saw Roy scoot in his chair and sit up, revealing a very bloodied shirt…definitely, not from a bloody nose.

"Here…here's your drink." He set it down on the counter. "I'm going to close out this couple's tab and then I'll be back. I want to hear about your promotion."

"Sounds like a plan, Stan." Roy let out a sloppy laugh.

Cody went to the cash register, printed out a receipt, wrote down a little something, then handed it to the couple.

The couple looked up at Roy, who "cheered" them with a goofy smile, then drank his drink as if it were water. The couple gave a curt nod then left the building.

Cody came back to Roy, with another drink.

"Ahh. See, I knew you'd want to celebrate with me." Roy patted the counter so Cody knew right where to place the glass.

"Of course. So, please, continue your story."

"Right, where was I?" Roy reached for his glass but retracted to scratch his back.

"The underdog…"

"Yes. The underdog placed her little name in the hat." He picked up his glass only to put it back down and reached around his back again. "Hold on. This thing is bugging the piss out of me." Reaching around his back again, Roy pulled out a gun, and tossed it to the side, hitting the wall as it slid down the counter.

Cody's heart fluttered, but he did his best to remain calm and engaging. "So, this underdog?"

Roy guzzled back the drink then slammed it on the counter. "Another, kind sir." Roy smiled with his eyes half open and hung his head as if he were bowing.

"Coming up." Cody took the glass and got another one.

"Vivian Sanders was her name. Young, 'bootiful', and…cunning. That's a good word. Cunning. This little minx had it out for me, you know? She hadn't been there long at all. And so I wondered…" Roy cleared his voice and changed it to impersonate the voice he had imagined in his head. A goofy lower tone than his normal voice. "Where did this girl come from? Why was she coming for my partnership?" He emphasized the last 'p' in the last word and spat a bit.

Cody gave Roy the drink.

Another one down the hatch. "Hey, Cody. Catch!" Roy tossed the glass up into the air and rolled over in laughter, hitting his forehead on the counter.

Cody lunged forward and caught the glass. He put it in the sink and very, very slowly began to make another.

Once Roy recovered from his giddy collision with the counter and continued, "So, I go into work yesterday, right? The big announcement day." He arched his stretched out arms over his head. "Mr. Thomas Vanderson…he is the big boss…walks into the conference room and winks. He winks at Ms. Sanders with this sly smile. Then he looks at me, removing the smile to a deadpan face and gives a curt nod. I knew then that I had lost it."

"Oh, no."

"Oh, no, is right, my friend. How is that drink coming along?"

Cody poured the Jim Beam into the glass. "Here you are."

"Cheers." Down, down, down it went.

"Then what happened?"

"Well, you know, he made his announcement. Everyone looked at me as they did a slow clap that gradually sped up so that they didn't appear to be rude. I went about my day questioning all my life decisions. And at the end of the day, I went home…but…today was a new day, or so I told myself. I decided to confront Mr. Bossman about his decision but didn't want to make a scene at work. So…Can I get another?"

Cody glanced at the man's withered stature and then at the gun. "Yes. I'll grab another for you." He began mixing and out of the corner of his eye he saw shadows getting into position outside. Cody drew in a small sigh of relief then continued making the drink.

"So, I stayed after work and waited in the main lobby downstairs. I made certain that I was the last one in the building, besides Thomas. I went back up to the offices and knocked on his door, but I went in before waiting for permission." Roy started chuckling. "Now, who do you suppose I saw? Hmm? Take a wild guess."

"Mr. Bossman?"

Roy blurted out laughter to the point he had tears in his eyes. "Very good. That's exactly right. Mr. Bossman's pale ass butt with none other than Ms. Minx Vivian Sanders with her skirt hiked up onto her ass, pounding away like little jackrabbits."

Cody handed Roy the drink.

Roy just held it. The tears of laughter that had welled up dripped down his face. "Cody. I don't know what came over me. Really. But I charged at him as he turned around and attempted to pull up his pants. I kneed him in the groin and slapped her across the face making her fall to the side. She hit her head on the desk. Blood started oozing out immediately. Thomas flung himself at me, taking me down to the ground. You know I was on the wrestling team in high school and college? I choked him out, but I didn't let go. I didn't let go." Roy drank his drink in a couple gulps between sobs.

Cody, with a slightly confused, yet mortified look on his face, once again, glanced at the gun sitting on the counter.

"Don't worry. There aren't any bullets. I sat in his office for quite a while. Partly to see if either of them would magically get up and partly because I had no idea what to do. I looked in his desk and found that, but…" His sobs and laughter were hard to distinguish at this point. "I couldn't find the bullets. So, I came here. My plan 'B', if you will. And you played your part with honor, dear Cody."

Cody's mouth was agape, eyes wide, and head tilted in confusion.

"Can you go outside for me? I believe we have some guests and they would like to talk to me. But do me a favor. Don't tell them about the gun." He gave a weepy smile and winked. "Go ahead. And thank you."

Cody slowly backed away out of the bar, with his hands up just to ensure he didn't get shot. As soon as he was in the clear, and the door closed, police readied themselves.

Cody tried yelling, "He's unarmed. There's no bullets!"

But it was too late. Bang.

The next day, the front news story was of a man named Roy McAndrews. Cody's statement had been released in the article. The headline read, "Suicide by Police After Murder".

THE THIRTEENTH SACRIFICE

To be dead was a unique novelty, one Silas Grant hadn't thought much about until the opportunity presented itself. After a near escape from the police, Silas gave into the fact that burning his house to the ground in order to conceal evidence of his "alleged" crimes was the only way he could continue his mission.

It was a mission he thought to have been passed down to him by a higher power though he wasn't entirely sure on which particular deity had sent him on such a quest. He just had this compelling notion to carry out all of his indiscretions and his deity had now granted him permission.

And so now, just after dawn when the fog rises a few inches above the tall, swampy grasses, Silas stood before his tomb located in the perpetually flooding Louisiana.

They had done a magnificent job with it. Clean, white marble—the placard on its face—sheened with a thin layer of the humid, late afternoon mist as a storm had just passed through. Flowers had even been planted around the area—a few rose bushes and some sorrowful lilies.

This was his first time seeing it after his funeral when he had hidden behind another tombstone close by. There had been a small parade that gathered, then he watched as a coffin was tucked away inside the tomb. It pained him to break from his utmost and honorable duties, but he knew that in order to continue his future endeavors he would have to go underground for some time.

Now, six months later, Silas had returned and was determined to complete what he had started. To say this would get messy would be an understatement, but the sacrifice was worth the reward. The reward—being able to walk amongst the most powerful gods of all—the ability to become a higher power himself.

A caw echoed, bouncing off the tombs. The crow landed on his crypt. It cawed again, locked eyes with Silas, then cocked its head.

"You can't kill a dead person. Best move on." Silas cracked a grin so sly, the devil himself would have blushed. After a peck or two at the structure, the crow fluffed out his wings and flew away. "And so it begins…again."

Silas pulled up his hood from his jacket, kicked up the kickstand on his motorcycle, and revved away. On his way out of town, he stopped at a red light. A young lady, in her twenties, had dropped her purse in the crosswalk. Silas got off his bike and trotted towards her.

"Oh. Thank you so much. My strap broke."

"Glad I could help." Silas picked up all the purse's contents then walked her to the sidewalk. "My name is Silas. Silas Grant." He offered his hand after the purse had been deemed in recovery.

"Margaret, but everyone calls me Maggie."

"Pleasure to meet someone so stunning and…fresh."

Maggie tilted her head ever so slightly, but blushed. "Oh, my. Well, the pleasure is all mine. Chivalry is hard to come by these days."

"Indeed."

The moment might have grown silent, but "awkward" wouldn't have been the phrase Silas would have used…- more like…mouthwatering, to see her squirm.

"Listen. I don't do this often, but I feel something here…a spark if you will. Can I take you for dinner and a drink? I have a helmet for you and I know the perfect place just outside of town."

"Hmm. I should say, 'no'."

"Maybe so."

"But…."

"Yes?"

"How could I resist such a tempting offer from the one who saved me and my purse?" Maggie giggled and looked down at her toes. She could feel them wiggling in her heels with adrenaline.

Silas handed Maggie the helmet to which she placed on her head then straddled Silas with her legs, securing her biking position.

After a few minutes, the street lights faded behind them as did the town. Without any warning, Silas hand-cuffed Maggie's wrists that had been hugging him, ensuring that she would stay in that vulnerable position.

Finally, they reached their destination. Maggie's throat hurt from the screaming, attempting to alert someone to her rescue; unfortunately though, they were quite alone.

Silas raised her tied hands over his head and got off the bike, never letting go of Maggie, as he knew she'd attempt an escape. Not that he complained. He admired a little fight in his sacrifices. He forcibly helped her off the bike and pulled her along down the path.

They were in the woods. A lake or some kind of water was near as Maggie could hear the trickling. After about a mile down a very bumpy path, if you could call it that, she could see a cabin. It seemed awfully small, and quite unkempt. Boards were coming off the siding; there were a couple of cracked windows, and the amount of debris on the roof and in the gutters was appalling.

The inside left much to be desired as well. There were holes in the flooring—creeks with every step—and the dust and grime on the surfaces made Maggie scrunch her tear-soaked face. And then there was the smell. The air was foul indeed. She couldn't quite pinpoint it, but it was quite unique. It was stale, stagnate air, but also smelled of mildew and spoiled food.

They walked up to a door, the only solid and stable thing there. While still holding onto Maggie with one hand, he grabbed a strap of leather that hung around his neck, at the end of which held a key. He unlocked the door and they ventured down a questionable staircase; all the while, the smell grew increasingly more putrid. There was a light flickering in the middle of the room.

Silas looked at Maggie with a creepy, grinning-clown intensity as he flicked on the lights. Maggie turned her head to view what was in front of her. Even though her throat hurt and her voice was raspy, she screamed at the top of her lungs, for sitting before her was an oblong-shaped table with fourteen chairs staged around it.

The head chair, opposing their current placement in the room, was empty and so were the two on either side of it. In the eleven other chairs, sat people…corpses all at various points of decomposition. Some still had some skin and hair—you could even make out faint facial features—while others were nothing but bone.

Maggie ran out of breath and passed out. Silas caught her then propped her up in the seat to the left of the empty head chair, and proceeded to tie her up.

As she gained consciousness, Maggie's neck was riddled with pain since her head was drooped while she was passed out. She carefully picked it up and blinked her eyes a couple times to allow them to adjust to her new environment. The smell of her surroundings shocked her yet again, making her chair wobble slightly as she attempted to free herself from the nightmare.

Silas witnessed her fit, but paid no mind to it. Instead, he continued to cut his steak and shovel food into his mouth.

Though still panicked, she knew she wasn't getting anywhere, so she took some breaths to try to calm herself. The repugnant odor consumed her senses and only served as a reminder of her environment, so she resorted to tears of anger and fear, knowing perfectly well it wasn't going to help the situation either, but it seemed to be all she could do.

Silas finished every last bite of his steak, potatoes, salad, and bread roll. He picked up his plate, went upstairs, and returned with a fresh one. He then placed it in front of Maggie.

"I can feed you, if you are hungry." Silas began cutting her steak.

Maggie looked up at him with a scowl.

"Suit yourself. It is the only way you will be able to eat. Just let me know."

Maggie's stomach had been aching with hunger, but there was no way in hell she would allow herself to stoop to that level. *If he is offering to feed me, then he obviously needs me for something. I'm sure to find a way out by then…right?*

Maggie woke the next morning to the sound of the cellar door slamming closed. Determined to not show him that he had won, she promised herself not to cry, and to once again turn down food.

"Are you ready for breakfast?" Silas came down and sat next to her. Oddly enough, there wasn't a plate of eggs or anything.

Questioning the lack of breakfast food, Maggie didn't answer and simply stared in front of her.

"That's fine. I'll be right back with my breakfast. We can at least sit together."

He stood back up, but before he took the first step up, Silas turned around, "I'll be having eggs, bacon, and a bowl of fruit. Unfortunately, your only option is the food you have in front of you. You chose not to eat your dinner last night and so it becomes your breakfast. Just thought I'd mention that."

Maggie strived to keep her astonishment behind a poker face, but given Silas' slimy smile, she gathered she had failed at the task.

Silas marched upstairs to ready his food. The smell of bacon faintly trailed down. It smelled good, but was quickly overpowered by the stench of her other unfortunate table guests.

"I can only imagine what is in store for me. I am so sorry you all fell victim to him. I just hope I can manage to get out and find justice for you all."

"I see you are meeting the others." Silas made his way back to the table with a plate full of food.

Maggie's stomach grumbled. There was no way he didn't hear her speaking with the others, but he ignored it just the same.

Silas pointed to the corpse next to her. "That is Laura. She was a librarian. She was reading a book about serial killers. It was a sign from the higher power. Katherine, next to her, was a teacher. She was getting coffee one morning. Joyce…," he continued going around the room. Each woman had a story and a life that he just took away from them. "I just bumped into her on the street. Isabella was beautiful. You can see how beautiful her face was given her cheek bones, right?"

Maggie couldn't help the tears streaming down her face.

"It is rude not to make eye contact, Margaret. I need you to look at Isabella, please."

Maggie didn't move and she muffled her sobs to the best of her ability.

"Damn it, I said look!" He stood up and grabbed her hair and pulled it back, treating her much like a puppet on a string.

She let out a yelp.

"Thank you. Heidi and Finley, on either side of Gloria—she was the first—are actually twins. I felt so lucky that night. Gloria, as I said, was my first and then to find the twins…I thought this process would go by so quickly. I enjoyed our time together. The three of them lasted quite awhile, but when they attempted to escape…." He shook his head and sat back down in his seat.

Maggie was forced to keep her head up; her scalp was throbbing from the yank.

"But, I learned from my mistakes and decided to have one at a time from then on though, I have my eyes set on the thirteenth already. So who knows…maybe you'll get a companion…as long as you keep your strength long enough and eat. But again, that is up to you. Now, where was I?"

Thinking she had to answer, Maggie in a cracked voice replied, "Heidi, Finley, and Gloria." She broke into quiet sobs as saying their names made it all the more real.

"Right. Glad you were paying attention. Evelyn was a tricky one. Danielle and Carly were best friends, but to ensure I didn't go against my rule, I took Danielle first. When she was in her last day or so, I took Carly. They saw each other for a few hours before Danielle sacrificed herself. And that leaves us with Beth. I almost got caught with her. That's why I had to fake my own death, play dead for six months, and resurrect like the Messiah that I was meant to be to complete my mission. That's why you are here."

Silas finished his meal with a swig of orange juice then glanced over at Maggie, who was still sobbing in the position that she was brutally put in.

"Are you sure you aren't hungry?"

"No, thank you."

"At least have some water. You'll whither away without it."

Maggie was extremely thirsty. Her lips were chapped and her mouth was like a desert. But could she live with herself if she begged for water from someone like Silas Grant? *Could I live without it?*

Maggie nodded against her better judgment.

Silas, all too pleased to play house with his new doll, ran upstairs only to return with a small glass of water.

"Drink it all, Maggie." Silas placed the rim of the glass to her lips and tilted her head back ever so gently.

Maggie took her few gulps and drank it all, relieving her sore throat for the time being.

"Good girl. Now, I have to run out and do some errands, but I'll be back for dinner."

After about an hour, Maggie fell asleep.

Silas went into town on his bike to stalk his new victim. He hadn't learned her name yet, but he planned to learn it today.

The woman was beautiful—black hair, hazel eyes, and tall but proportioned all around. The perfect final sacrifice. She looked familiar, but he couldn't place her. He had spotted her in the graveyard. She had been visiting a tomb, but the name on the tomb didn't ring any bells either.

Silas went to his crypt again. The day was rainy and the fog that morning had been dense. But like clockwork, the woman was spotted on the grounds, a few tombs down. She seemed focused, and yet a sorrow hovered over her.

He plucked a couple of the flowers around his tomb and waltzed over to her.

"I've seen you here before. I'm sorry for your loss." He handed her the flowers.

"Thank you."

She smelled them and smiled briefly.

"My name is Silas."

"Oh. Like the placard named over there?" She pointed to his grave.

Silas' heart skipped a beat. He hadn't expected such a response, so he had to think on his feet if she was to be the last piece to his puzzle. "Yes. My father. We have the same name."

"I'm terribly sorry for your loss, Silas."

"Thank you." For the first time, Silas had been caught off guard with a potential victim. He cleared his throat. "Your name?"

"My, where are my manners? I am Alice, Alice Copper."

"Alice. What a perfect name."

"I do believe so."

"Might I be so bold as to ask what you are doing for dinner tonight?"

"I have plans for tonight. But, tomorrow I think I am free. Where did you have in mind?"

"I have a place just out of town that has great food and an even better atmosphere."

"That sounds great. I can meet you here around six tomorrow evening?"

"I will see you then, Alice."

As proper as any southern belle would, she nodded her gratitude to Silas and made her way back to the gravel path leading out of the cemetery.

Maggie woke with a jolt to her stomach writhing in twists and turns. She had already relieved herself a few times but the thought of doing more than the already degrading urine sample was a mortifying possibility. She craved to curl up into a ball, arms holding her stomach together as it seemed as if it was going to split open, but her arms were tied to the chair's arm rests and her ankles tied to its legs. All she could accomplish was to curl over, resting her head on the table in front of her.

Sooner than she wanted, she heard Silas return, his footsteps striking terror into every atom of her being. He didn't come downstairs right away, but Maggie could hear the clanking of pots and pans. She squirmed in her soaked seat, debating whether she should even bother asking to use a toilet—not knowing which was worse, asking for assistance from a sadist or messing oneself.

Unfortunately, the urge was too great, and the need for some civilization should be expected.

"Silas!" She yelled through gritted teeth and against her better judgment. "Silas!"

He came down. "How can I help, Maggie?"

"My stomach. Can I use the toilet?" Her face was scrunched in pain.

"Umm. I'll tell you what. Since you asked fairly nicely, I will get a bedpan, help you lift your clothes, and you can go in that."

A groaned sigh escaped her mouth.

"I'm afraid that is all I can offer at the moment. Removing you from the seat itself is out of the question, and I don't think you'd want me to cut a hole in the bottom with you still sitting on it? No. I didn't think so. I'll get you that bedpan."

If Maggie could cry she would, but at this moment, she didn't see the point.

He returned with a bedpan, then had her lean forward and stand slightly so that he could slide the pan under her. He then proceeded to unbutton her pants and shimmy them down to her knees.

Maggie's shirt hung over her waist, enough so if she were to sit, her shirt would be messed. The ever-so-thoughtful Silas recognized the problem and removed her shirt all together for her, revealing her black laced bra.

Instead of leaving Maggie with some kind of privacy, Silas stayed and watched and listened to her as she could no longer hold it in. All Maggie could do was look away.

Once there was a brief pause, he went upstairs, leaving her the most vulnerable she had ever felt in her life. He returned with his plate of food, got her dressed and removed the bedpan.

There was no choice of water for the night, as Silas insisted on it. Given his determination with it, Maggie suspected it to be the cause of her stomach issues. And now that her stomach was completely emptied, she caved and asked for a few bites of food.

Even though she had been watching flies and gnats land on the food for a day now, her will to survive was strong enough to choke some down.

"What will you have first? How about some potatoes?"

She nodded.

He smiled. Silas stabbed a squishy red potato with a fork and brought it up to her mouth.

She parted her lips just enough for it to fit and he jammed it in her mouth.

"Now, chew thoroughly and swallow. Don't you dare spit it out. That would be rude."

Gagging, she did as she was told.

He stabbed another potato and proceeded this way until all the potatoes were gone.

"I'm full." Her skin tone took on a greenish hue.

"As you wish. Wash it down with some water."

She started to turn her head.

"Be rude and I'll make you eat the whole plate instead of giving you a fresh plate tomorrow morning."

As if it were a reward, Maggie drank the rest of her suspected poisonous water.

Silas walked next to her, bent down, and kissed her on the cheek, then retired upstairs.

Through the night, Maggie did nothing but toss and turn as her bowels were unforgiving and Silas either didn't care about her wailing or found some sick kind of joy in it.

Breakfast the next morning was silent. Silas obviously had something occupying his mind, and Maggie simply didn't have the courage or strength to chat. He did seem gracious enough to give her some of his eggs off of his plate, which Maggie truly saw as a treat.

"Finish up breakfast with your water and then I'll put you into something a bit more presentable. We will have another guest joining us tonight."

Again, being too weak to fight, she drank the water.

Silas then proceeded to undress her, minus her shirt as that would require untying her at some point, cleaned up the chair and floor around her, then braided her hair. This time he left the bedpan under her so that nothing would be out of place when the new arrival came.

"I'll be back for dinner. Try to get some rest. Tonight is a big night. The night when all my hard work will pay off. I'll need you to look and act your best."

Maggie nodded.

"Sorry, didn't quite catch that."

"Yes, sir."

"Good." And he left. Once again leaving Maggie's thoughts spinning in her head of what was to come.

Silas parked his bike on the sidewalk just outside the cemetery gate. His groceries for the evening were secured to his storage bags that hung on either side of the back of his motor bike.

As he walked through the iron gates, he saw Alice walking towards him…again, unexpected. He was growing tired of the surprises she kept throwing his way, but was able to navigate past this one just as well as the others. She was carrying something in her hands.

"Did you give up on me that easily? I believe I am here right on time?" Silas glanced at his watch and verified his precise timing.

"I figured you'd be here promptly, so I figured I'd meet you at the gates."

"How courteous. And you brought flowers for the evening."

"Mhmm. Some of my favorites. Queen Anne's lace and these purple ones are violets and I threw in some greenery. They are from my personal garden."

"How thoughtful." He looked at the very familiar plants and wondered if she was trying to play him or if she was just daft. Either way, it made her all the more interesting to him. "Shall we? I have my bike."

"Lovely. I've never been on one before. How exhilarating."

"Here is a helmet."

"I'm fine. I don't want to mess up my hair."

"Suit yourself. Climb on."

Alice did as she was told and hugged him with the flowers in front.

They drove out of town, but he couldn't manage to restrain her with the flowers in the way. They kept driving, but he thought of a plan. Before turning down his road, he pulled over to the side.

"It is kind of difficult to see down the next few roads. Would you mind if I put the flowers in the back with the groceries?"

"Well…umm."

Her hesitation clued him into the fact that she knew what she held was a bouquet of poisonous flowers.

"Or how about we just get rid of them all together?" He ripped the flowers out of her hands and threw them into the ditch. "Your Queen Anne's Lace is a bit more umbrellaed than it is supposed to be. I think you planted the wrong plant. The fact that you had hemlock in that means you know enough about me to want me dead, clever enough to know that I faked my death, and yet stupid enough to attempt to follow through with killing me yourself. My only question now is why?"

Alice clenched her jaw. There was so much she wanted to say to him but now wasn't the time.

Silas grabbed her arm and handcuffed them together, then got her on the bike. While holding on to her, he sat in front and locked her in. They turned down the road.

Both got out and began their mile walk to the cabin. She stayed in front of him the whole time, secretly fidgeting with her arms. She decided to run for it, running towards the cabin.

She tripped up the cabin steps and rolled onto her back to fight if needed. When he leaned down to pick her up, she jabbed him with a syringe then scratched his neck.

Silas let go and stumbled back just enough to allow Alice to get herself up and go into the cabin. She found the door, and using the key that she had just snatched from his neck, opened the door.

Alice ran downstairs and discovered the terror that sat before her.

Maggie groggy, but alert enough to realize that this was out of the ordinary and in her favor, perked up the best she could.

"We need to act fast. I poisoned him with strychnine but it'll take a few more minutes to kick in. In my back pocket, I have a razor blade. Grab it for me."

Alice turned and squatted a bit so that Maggie could grab it with her tied up wrists.

The running thumps of Silas echoed like a ticking time bomb.

"Hurry." Alice turned back around when she felt Maggie's fingers lift the blade out of her pocket. Alice grabbed it and began to cut away at Maggie's hand ropes. "You'll have to get your feet. You think you can do that?"

Maggie nodded.

Alice got one hand free.

Silas all but fell downstairs, rushing to stop them. "You are not getting away. You are trapped…nowhere to go."

Maggie continued to cut her restraints.

Alice, determined to distract him, started walking around the table.

Then, he saw it. Alice was right next to Isabella. "You…you're related, aren't you? What was she? A sister, cousin…? No…a daughter. You both have those striking cheekbones. So, how did you determine that my death was fake?"

"My husband was on the fire team that put out your house fire. He said that the body that was found looked too old for it to be you, but the media wanted the chaos you had caused to be put to rest, and the public officials agreed. I went to your funeral. I saw you peeking behind the old man's tomb where you had stolen the body."

"I was gone for so long. Why wait until now to seek your revenge?"

Maggie, now both hands free, moved to her feet. Silas seemed uninterested in her as he was involved with his new play thing.

Silas began to feel aches and pains in his legs and arms, and his breath was getting faint.

"You truly disappeared. I lost track of you. But I went to the cemetery every day. I knew you'd be back. And sure enough, there you were. You found me, as I had hoped, and I found you. I gave myself a day to ensure all my things were in order and talk to the police chief. His daughters were taken as well."

"Aww. The twins."

"He is on the way to get you. I just gave us a head start by giving you a cocktail to slow you down."

Silas was getting more agitated. He had been bested. *This can't be the end.* His jaw tightened and each breath became more and more faint. He collapsed, reaching out for Maggie who finally got herself free from the chair.

Sirens wailed. Maggie made her way to Alice's side. No longer able to be in the same room as those whom he had murdered before, they went upstairs.

The chief greeted them at the door.

"He's down there?" The chief's eyes were filled with a hateful sorrow.

Alice responded simply, "Yes."

Alice took Maggie outside where the EMTs could take her to the hospital and begin treatment for the poison.

Alice stood outside. Another cop uncuffed her, then everyone heard a shot coming from the house. Then another one, and another, and another. The chief emerged, then vomited over the decrepit porch banister.

The following morning, Maggie woke to Alice's nurturing face.

"You saved me." Maggie began to tear up.

"Don't you cry, at least not for long. Don't you give him that satisfaction."

"What will happen to him? Jail?"

Alice shook her head. "I wasn't lying when I said the twins were the chief's daughters. When you left in the ambulance last night, the chief showed Silas the same respect he had shown all of his victims. At the end...." Alice checked the door to ensure that the deputy who was watching over her wasn't eavesdropping. "He shot him—in the knee, his shoulder, his manhood, then his head. He can't hurt you anymore. He can't hurt anyone anymore."

The release of muscle tension that Maggie had been holding left with a sigh so satisfying that she was actually able to form a smile.

Alice held her hand. "It's all over, Maggie. It's all over."

THE THIRTEENTH CANDLE

Standing in front of a full-length mirror was a young girl with plain features. She had gray eyes and nearly ashen skin, and she was wearing an all black dress with her light brown hair tied back into a very low ponytail. After adjusting—more like pulling her collar away from her neck—she shuffled to her little window in her room where the moon, though only a sliver, smiled at her. The stars twinkled and even the crickets hummed her a tune.

"Allegra…."Her mom knocked, then opened the door. "Are you ready? The ceremony will start soon. It's almost midnight."

"I guess so." Allegra shrugged then lowered her gaze.

"Come sit with me." Jade sat on her daughter's bed. "What's the matter? You've been looking forward to this day for some time now. Why the sorrowful look?"

Allegra sat down next to her mom and sighed. "I don't know. What if I don't get an elemental specialty like cousin Sarah?"

"Your cousin Sarah's was simply delayed. Sometimes it can be hard for the 'Mother' to choose which gift a witch was meant to give. In your cousin's case, her strongest elements were water and fire. Given that fire is rare, as it should only be given to those who can control their emotions, the 'Mother' wanted to wait another few years to see her potential."

Allegra didn't seem to find much comfort in her mom's words.

Jade nudged Allegra's shoulder. "If you ask me, I think she'll be a water."

"Like Aunt Cordelia?"

"Exactly."

"Can you tell me the story again? About Madam Rosalind."

Jade looked at her clock. "I suppose we have just enough time."

Allegra turned onto her belly, chin in hands, and gazed in wonder at her mom.

"Many centuries ago, a woman sought refuge in the woods from hunters who were told by a man whom she had refused relations with, that she was a witch. Finally, with no one in sight, she leaned over to take a few moments and breathe. Suddenly, she heard voices and the rustling of leaves as her hunter grew nearer. There was no way she could move from where she was without giving her position away. She thought she had been caught, but all she could do was stay put.

"They were surrounding her, but no one seemed to actually see her. It was as if they were looking past her. Finally, the hunters dispersed, having given up on finding her, even though she was in plain sight. She looked around and finally down at the ground surrounding her. She had been in a mushroom circle, and beside her, in its center, grew a tall, single, black rose tinged with golden dust along the petals' edges, which opened into a full bloom as the moon's light kissed it.

"The woman took it as a sign that someone in this otherwise cruel world was watching over her. This time, when she heard the noises again, she wasn't as startled, and as she looked around, she saw a wolf with glowing green eyes. Its paws planted firmly and with purpose, then it bowed.

"Cautiously, the woman walked toward it; it raised its nose to the palm of her hand when she reached out, and she swore she heard the wolf say, 'Rosalind'. The woman, by instinct, knew that she had a new name—one bound to the earth, its roots, and to this creature now before her.

"Rosalind, in turn, named the wolf 'Midnight', as the moon was at its peak.

"That week, she took shelter in the woods that had saved her life, and to her surprise, several other women had wandered to the very same place. They created the first coven—our coven—and called themselves 'The Midnight Roses'."

With a confused look, Allegra sat up onto her feet. "What was her name before Rosalind?"

"No one knows. But for generations after, we have received our first name by the 'Mother' via our familiars. Your name that we call you now will become your middle name."

"So your middle name is Helena?"

"Yes. That is the name that my mom, your grandma, gave me when I was born. Then for my thirteenth birthday, my rabbit, Fern, told me my name given to me by our 'Mother' goddess was Jade. I am an earth witch. Your Aunt Cordelia-Martha is a water witch. She has the cutest little river otter named Wells. Your grandmother Aura-Morgan is of air and has a crow named Esen, and your great-grandmother had a cat. I can't remember the cat's name, but your great-grandmother's name was Thora-Cecilia, and she was also an air witch."

"Who was the last fire witch?"

"Most of the coven believes that the last one was one of the original women in the woods, but no one knows much about her. The whole history of the fire witch has always been a bit of a mystery. There were whispers when I was growing up, before I got my gift, that there had been a fire witch, but that she turned too far to dark magic and ended up setting a grove of trees on fire, and then she vanished."

Allegra's stomach fluttered with butterflies. She grimaced then forced a breath.

Jade gently picked up her daughter's chin with her finger. "You have absolutely nothing to worry about, my dear. You have a kind heart, a beautiful soul, and a strength in both your powers and your will that I have never seen before. You will be just fine."

Allegra's breath eased and she let out a sigh.

"Are you ready?"

Allegra smiled and touched the floor with her bare feet.

Jade and Allegra were the last ones to appear at the clearing. The whole coven had turned up in support of the new witch. Each had a cloak of her elemental gift worn over their black dresses. Allegra clenched her mom's hand before parting ways; Jade stopped to complete the circle and Allegra continued walking to the altar in the center.

There were just enough torches on the outskirts of the coven's circle to provide light for fellow witches to see each other, but the long walk to the glowing altar was a daunting and dark one.

Finally, Allegra made it to the center. The stone slab housed offerings from each element facing a different direction: feathers in the North, a water lily in the West, soil in the East, and ash in the South. Surrounding each offering were three candles marked with their respective elemental symbol. A thirteenth candle sat in the center and directly in front of Allegra.

"I call upon the elemental powers of the goddess 'Mother'. I ask…" Allegra's stomach bubbled. She forced air out from her mouth and gulped hard. "I ask, if it pleases her, that she bless me with a gift. Whether it be—air, water, earth, or fire—I offer myself to be only of service to others in need while in possession of such a gift, for my life is no better than any other's soul."

After mere seconds of utter silence, the wind picked up, circling the altar and Allegra. The earth trembled and water pooled from the soil, lifting up and hovering at Allegra's eye level. The candles flickered. Allegra, thriving on the energy of the chaos around her, pushed herself forward a couple steps to the center candle and blew out its flame.

Everything stopped. The winds died down, the droplets fell back to the earth and settled on the once again solid ground. Looking back at the altar to see which set of candles were still lit, she saw all had been blown out by the wind. As logical as this was, it wasn't supposed to happen. All the candles were supposed to have gone out except for the appointed elemental candles signifying her gift.

Is this what happened with cousin Sarah? Allegra looked back at her mom for a sign that everything would be alright.

Jade bowed her head. Then so did the witches on either side of her. This continued in its entirety, then Allegra finally noticed why. All the candles were sparking like celebratory sparklers, but only for a few moments.

Suddenly, all the candles went dark, minus the three on the fire altar. Those roared with a magnitude of light and heat. She thought she should be covering her eyes or shielding her face, and yet the flames captured her attention, drawing her into the flame's dance. Allegra's heartbeat fluttered as fast as a hummingbird's wings. Her brow increasingly got hotter. Her head felt light. After her eyes rolled back, and as she fell to the ground, what looked to be a stray ember latched itself onto Allegra and set her aflame.

There was nothing around Allegra except darkness and the smallest flicker of light in the distance. Slowly, but with unwavering strength, the light came closer. Soon it was close enough for her to see that the light was a flame. And as the flame got closer, it got bigger. When it stopped in front of Allegra, a woman stepped from it. The flame died to a mere glow in a sea of blackness around them. Her dress was long and so were her delicate black sleeves.

"Allegra. You have been chosen to be fire reincarnated, for you are a flame born again from the ashes."

"Who are you?" Allegra felt no fear, no flutters in her stomach, just a curious strength she hadn't felt before.

"I am Fire. Though most will know me as Nina or Tana. I was there in the beginning with sister Rosiland, and again two years ahead of your mother."

Allegra's thoughts were everywhere. She hadn't remembered any other witch talking about ancestors coming to talk to them as they received their gifts. She also felt hot enough to be a flame herself, and yet she felt comfort in the heat of it all.

"Fire is a rare gift. It is not scientifically everlasting as the other elements are. Air is all around us as it is what gives us life. Earth is what holds us up, and water sustains our beings and is the majority of our makeup. Tell me…what happens to something when you set it on fire?"

"It crumbles to ash."

"Exactly. Fire isn't always around; therefore, it must be recycled or reincarnated, born again. But this can't be given to just anyone…"

The woman walked around Allegra, not to intimidate, but to become familiar. "Like Nina, with the original coven, our powers, though great, were new—not just to us, but to the world as we knew it. Goddess Mother did assist, but as there was no history, mistakes were made often. Because fire can destroy, those mistakes had great costs for Nina. No one really knows what happened to her, but I can tell you what happened with me. You see…I had a love, and being as young as I was and a novice in my craft, you can only imagine how well I handled finding him sharing another woman's bed.

"The passion I had for him turned to a dark hatred, and I accidently set the room aflame, trapping him, her, and myself in it. We all perished…only for me to come back generations later, when Goddess Mother felt the need for another chance for redemption. You see, the elements were beginning to sway; the balance had been askew long enough.

"And so Tana was born. She handled the gift with great pride. She was a true fighter, a hero to our cause. Unfortunately, her fight would cost her her life. Tana was protecting the coven with a wall of fire from witch hunters who had trapped the coven. She held onto her flame for as long as she could. Days had passed, until she quite literally burnt out. Her wall of fire held on long enough after her soul had left to chase the hunters away, giving the coven the chance to seek shelter. And now, the coven uses that very same clearing as their most sacred land.

"When the coven had returned to recover their dead, Tana's body was nowhere to be found. All that was left was ash…until now. You are the next witch of fire. You are the rebirth of strength, a fierce love and power that, at some point, will fade, be reabsorbed, and recycled when a fresh start is needed again. Though I cannot tell you how long until that is, I can say that you are the vessel needed for the balance to be restored. Are you prepared to accept such a gift… and curse?"

Allegra was in complete awe of the knowledge and possible responsibility that was just thrown upon her. However, digging deep into her heart, feeling the serenity in this moment, she knew this to be her fate. How could she possibly deny the world, her coven, or herself that opportunity?

"I am."

The woman embraced Allegra and set her ablaze again.

The remaining ash that had been lying dormant in front of the weeping mother, Jade, began to swirl, forming a tornado which, in turn, sparked like a firework finale. A body appeared and lay on the ground, her body warm to the touch.

Allegra woke to see her mom. Jade was holding her hand and brushing her daughter's red-tinged brown hair to the side, revealing her red and golden flaked eyes.

"Allegra, are you alright?" Jade helped her sit up.

Allegra stood and as she did, the ash from the altar and the flame from the fire candles encased her once more, gracing her body with a striking red formal-length lace gown and a dark red cloak. Her cheeks warmed with a light natural blush. She had been transformed, both outside and within.

Allegra's once fluttering butterflies had turned to a slow burning brew of confidence that could be seen in the way she held herself, no longer hunched over, but standing with her head held high. "I am…I am fire."

Her eyes and red highlights in her hair began to glow red. What looked like a laser, engraved patterns on her hand and up her right arm. The lines intertwined to form a silhouette.

A yip from the tree line drew the attention of the coven; all eyes changed their focus. It was a creature. A creature that shared the same silhouette that just made its mark onto Allegra.

She and the creature walked towards each other. Their eyes both glowing with the same color. It was a fox. A beautiful, burnt-orange fox with a white chest and black paws and eartips. Its tail was fluffy, as most foxtails are; however, the color was unusual. It was red—bright, fiery red.

The fox yipped again, and though the coven heard just that, Allegra heard her new name. "Ember. A fire that keeps going."

In response, Ember-Allegra named her new companion, "Enya."

The two bowed to each other with the utmost respect, then playfully, the fox leaped into Ember's arms. They rejoined the coven to make their formal introductions and celebrate the new gift bestowed upon them.

The celebration continued until the following evening, when the horizon lost the last flicker of the fire-burning sun.

The Thirteenth Angel

Lucifer filled up his cup of doom and gloom as he did every morning. It never seemed to take the chill out of hell itself, but being Lucifer, it was still worth the grumble.

Anyway, Lucifer looked out of his tower's window. The moat around the castle connected to the River Styx. Lost souls dwelled in the waters while others were brought to the council and judged. Were they destined for hell, or were they granted to live in peace in a more heavenly place? Some could even receive the opportunity to try life again, to be reincarnated.

Lucie hadn't originally appreciated his assignment from his father, but when his twin brother, Bezaliel joined him, Lucifer found himself defending the underworld to him.

Lucifer sipped his lukewarm sludge and went into the living room where his brother had been waiting for him.

"Brother! What's the plan for today? And please, don't tell me it consists of sitting for hours on end listening to souls babble about their once mundane lives."

"Same morning, different day, Bezaliel. Like always. It's my job."

Bezaliel sighed an overly exaggerated sigh.

"Really, Bezaliel. It's not like I begged for you to come down here to rescue me or anything. Sure, it was lonely for a bit, but I would have managed. And don't get me wrong, I'm glad you're here, but it just doesn't seem to be your pace."

"Well, I wasn't expecting it to be so…so boring."

Lucifer blankly stared at his twin.

"I just want to travel. I guess I thought that getting away from the self-righteous side of the family and out of the gated jailhouse we called home, I'd be able to meet more people. And I'm not talking about listening to desperate people grasping at straws who only focus on their best moments. That isn't life. I want to know their highs and lows. That's what makes a person a person and shows a true life."

"How the hell would you know? You're an angel, not a human. Humans have souls, and their lives are based on their choices."

"Yes, and I'm an angel who CHOSE to come down here to support my brother. And I may not have a soul, but that doesn't mean I don't enjoy knowing more about humans. I like studying them—finding out what encourages their choices."

"I don't know what to tell you. You keep trying to change how things are. Are you trying to ascend and return to the place you once called home? Your wings will fry, and you'd be stuck on Earth forever—the fallen stay fallen, Brother."

"Fuck this. Mark me absent from today's festivities. I'm going to Earth to roam around and see whom I can meet."

Bezaliel stood from the cold, stone couch. He stretched out his arms, and his gray wings expanded double the size of his arm span. With a slight bend in his knees, Bezaliel took off out a nearby window and followed the River Styx upstream to the gates of hell.

As a fallen angel, he was allowed access in and out of the gates of hell without question. Cerberus, as always, barked at him on the way out. Bezaliel loved this thrill of escaping the cold, dark walls of his brother's home—to be nearer to the sun than he had since his falling—even though it had only been about a month, he yearned to feel its warmth.

Beginning his upward flight, he wondered if he would ever see his wings white again. He had been proud of the pristine white they once were, but even for the short time he had been sent as an outcast to the underworld, they had begun to tarnish and turn gray.

Finally, Bezaliel could feel the change in the air…the compassion versus the rejected. The tunnel increasingly narrowed. His feathers knocked off chunks of moist soil. Reaching out his arms, he clung to a root of a tree and retracted his wings. Bezaliel climbed up the last little bit, popping out under a willow tree next to a still lake.

After watching the next ferry to the underworld shove off, Bezaliel wandered. For hours, days, weeks, he watched the people around him. Though none could see him or communicate with him, he observed their connection to each other, how they communicated feelings of love, hate, and sadness. He witnessed the strength of their bravery and the ability to ask for forgiveness, in addition to the betrayal of slyly stabbing a friend in the back.

As he walked along the sidewalk one day, there was an older gentleman who caught his eye, almost quite literally. The man looked right at him. It was the first human to do so.

Bezaliel walked across the street to meet him. He sat down beside the man in silence, waiting to see if the man would start the conversation…if he could really see him.

The man was weathered, to put it nicely. His skin was wrinkled and tough as leather. His eyes were tired, as if he hadn't had a good night's sleep in years. He wore many layers of clothes, but Bezaliel imagined he was fairly fit or maybe even on the thin side. His facial hair was scruffy and patchy, and yet, even with all of that against him, his cheeks were still a bit rosy, and his eyes had enough of a twinkle left to give a sense of kindness to his aura.

"Well," the man grumbled in a scratchy deep voice, "are you going to just sit there or are you going to introduce yourself?"

Bezaliel looked around him. No one else was within ear shot. The man could see him. *How?* "I am Bezaliel."

"That's a mouthful. I think I'll call you Ben, if that's alright?"

"Sure. So, what's your name?"

"Jefferies. Colin Jefferies."

"Glad to make your acquaintance."

"I'm sure it is." Colin coughed. He politely covered his mouth with a hanky he pulled out of his almost ripped pocket. When he went to put it back, Bezaliel noticed splotches of blood stains. Some fresh from just now, but many brownish, from days ago.

"Are you alright, Mr. Jefferies? Can I get you some water?" Bezaliel leaned forward to stand, but was pulled back down by Colin.

"I'll be fine. Can I tell you a story?"

"Um. Sure."

"Right." Colin cleared his throat and wiped his mouth, ensuring that all the blood was removed from his lips. "When I was a boy, my brother and I would go into the woods behind our house and go on these pointless adventures. But it was the only time I really got to spend time with him as he was quite a few years older than me and had school activities and way more homework than I ever did. Anyway, one day we went out and I found this rabbit. It was a little thing. I guessed it was a baby, but I couldn't find its nest let alone its mother. Now, we had a coyote problem. My brother told me it was the circle of life and to let nature take its course, right? But..." Colin grabbed his handkerchief again and gripped his chest in addition to covering his mouth as he had another coughing spell.

"Excuse me. But I just couldn't let that happen. To let a life so young die such a painful and lonely death. I just couldn't do it. So I took it home, knowing perfectly well that my parents did not want another pet. We already had two dogs, a stray cat, and my brother's snake. But I pictured myself as that bunny. I wouldn't want the jaws of anything, least of all a coyote, around my neck. Once we got home, I put it up in my room, which I shared with my brother, and placed it in a shoebox under my bed, just until after dinner. Then I would find a more suitable environment for it."

"Sounds reasonable enough."

Colin's layers of clothes bubbled as he chuckled. "Yeah. I thought so too, until I ran back upstairs after clearing my plate from the table to find Brody's snake out of its cage—the tail of that slimy sucker sticking out from underneath the bed. Man, I cried for days over that little bunny. I did my best to rescue it from one horrible death only to hand it over to another death on a silver platter...well, a cardboard one anyway."

"That's terrible."

"It was. But what was worse was the fucked up logic I had learned from it. Everyone is going to die. And if it's their time, it's their time."

Bezaliel noticed water falling down Colin's cheek. He had heard about this. They were called tears. Tears were a naturally occurring liquid that expelled from the eyes due to happiness, anger, or, more commonly, sadness.

"After growing up a bit, I was drafted. Hell, I didn't think it at the time, but I was still a child then. And I'm sure you were busy during the war just as I was, fighting constantly with myself, probably more than I did our enemy—asking myself if my life was indeed more important than the guy's on the other side of my sight. Was he really that different from myself? And if I spared his life, would I simply be postponing the inevitable? Would me shooting him now, a solid hit to the head, be better than being captured, tortured, and eventually killed? Who was I to answer those questions? Who was I to pass such a judgment?"

Bezaliel was speechless. To watch the spirit of a man crumble before him—the pure sorrow emanating from his soul pierced Bezaliel like nothing before. He sank in his posture, as if a loaded burden had been thrown upon his shoulders.

"I wish there was something I could do to help you."

"Isn't that why you're here? To take me home?"

"Home?" Bezaliel had asked the question and yet he felt as if he already knew the answer. Was this his purpose?

"Home, Ben. Heaven. Hell. Any place that isn't here. I came back from that war a lifetime ago, and it haunts me. It changed me so much; I wasn't recognizable to my family when I came back." Colin coughed and wheezed over and over, gasping for a full inhale. Grabbing his chest, he fell backwards onto the sidewalk. His breaths were heavy and restricted.

Bezaliel picked him up, placing his head in his lap. "I'll take you home, Colin Jeffries."

Colin cracked a smile as a tear fell onto Bezaliel's robes. When Bezaliel lifted Colin, Colin's soul separated from his body. Bezaliel stretched out his wings and pushed off from the ground, watching Colin's body get smaller and smaller.

Passing the clouds, into the stars, and beyond what any human could imagine, the gates of heaven opened, with the Creator standing by.

"Bezaliel, you shouldn't be here…your wings?"

"My wings are of no concern at the moment. This soul was broken and it needs mending. It has seen enough sadness. I seek your judgment and your healing presence to give this soul a home."

"This is quite an unconventional request, Bezaliel. I'm not sure…."

"I am. Please, weigh his life and welcome him."

The Creator, still unsure, took the soul from Bezaliel's arms through the gates and weighed his heart. When the Creator came back, Bezaliel's wings were blackened. Was it the uncanny sorrow that he had been exposed to or the brightness of Heaven? He wasn't sure, but he was confident it was meant to be.

"He is at peace, Bezaliel. Now what to do with you? You can't come back here full-time."

"I wouldn't wish it. Nor do I wish to permanently live with Lucifer, bless him."

The Creator beamed at Bezaliel.

"You placed your worries aside to ensure safe passage for this soul. I believe that is your destiny. You are the Angel of Shadows, Bezaliel. You will make passage for those who are at their end, but not a moment too soon, waiting in the shadows until they have called for you. You can travel between all vails for the betterment of the soul."

Bezaliel nodded with reverence. "Thank you, Father." With a new sense of purpose, peace, and pride, Bezaliel leaned into a trust fall, spiraling down to Earth, sporting his new sleek, shadowed wings.

THE THIRTEENTH SOUL

Ashley peered out to the "backyard" from the garret. She could easily spy the sinister object that was stuck in the thick, wet sands of the marshy cove. The thought of selling this house yet again, only for the occupants to meet a tragic end, almost made Ashley feel sick to her stomach. It was the money they continued to make off of it that put her priorities in check. She only wished the Simms family would have picked high tide to tour the house.

After checking her watch and noticing the time, Ashley made haste downstairs, drew shut the curtains that would otherwise reveal the low-tide cove, and headed to the front door. The family would soon be here. As she stepped out the door, a breezy-blue Jeep revved up the street then turned into the driveway and came to an abrupt halt.

A man stepped out. He was wearing a white-collared, button-up shirt, dark denim pants, and had dark sunglasses covering his very fake-tanned face. After slamming his door, he raced over to the passenger side to open the door for his wife. She was dressed to the nines—not what you'd expect for a family looking at a beach house. She was wearing "peek-a-boo toe" red stilettos, a skimpy tight, red dress that barely kept her chest in position, and her hair was wrapped up as tight as one would imagine her personality to be.

The couple looked around the front of the property without a word to Ashley, who was waiting patiently on the porch. After a few brief moments, the woman yelled, "Paige, let's go. We haven't got all day. I have to be back at the office by three for a meeting."

The back passenger door of the Jeep opened. A girl, looking to be around fifteen or sixteen, hopped down from the seat and slammed the door.

"Easy on that door, young lady. We may be rich, but we don't want to waste it, right?" The man flashed his cheesy smile, finally acknowledging the realtor.

Ashley plastered a smile on her face and stepped forward, greeting the Simms family.

"You must be Cole and Martha Simms." Ashley offered her hand; unfortunately, both of them were still gazing at their phones, scrolling through emails, completely oblivious to the social graces extended before them.

"Yes, they are. And I am their offspring, Paige. My apologies for the zombies." Paige met the realtor's hand with a firm enough grip and rolled her eyes in the direction of her parents.

"Sorry about that. Can we head in and take a look?" Martha finally secured her phone in her clutch. "I have that meeting at three." She looked at her husband, nudged him with her pointy elbow, and gave him a look.

"Yes. Let's get on with it, shall we." He, too, slipped his phone into his back pocket, then stepped up onto the first step of the porch, letting himself lead the party in.

"Of course, after you." Ashley broke her grasp with Pagie and darted to the side so she wouldn't be bumped into by Cole.

No longer feeling guilty about selling the house to this couple, Ashley grinned as she followed them over the threshold.

It was your typical, recently renovated beach house and quaintly staged as such— the sturdiness of an older house with a more modern, bright, open concept. No doubt the Simms family, if they were to buy it, would ruin the charming decor with colder, spartan furnishings. The house featured three bedrooms, two and a half baths, a small cellar, the garret upstairs (which was finished but wasn't counted as one of the bedrooms), a fully updated kitchen, and your typical living room with a grand exit to the back porch and an attached boardwalk leading the way down to the water.

The members of the family scattered, exploring different rooms. While Paige's parents stayed on the main level, Paige wandered upstairs to the garret. It was quiet. Paige finally felt as though she could breathe without being told she was doing it wrong. In the corner of the room was a door—tall enough for a toddler to enter without having to crouch down. Paige, on the other hand, would have to duck under the door's frame to enter. The knob was the shape of a beautiful, round cut diamond.

With a quarter turn to the right, the door opened. A light invited Paige to ascend the small, iron-spiraling staircase. Once at the top, it opened up to a small deck—just enough room for one person and maybe a chair and side table—a decently sized widow's watch. The landing was fenced in with iron as well, and the view left Paige speechless. She closed her eyes and inhaled. The breeze of the salty air parted her strawberry-tinged brown hair, revealing her porcelain, delicate facial features with freckles that peppered her nose and cheeks. With an exhale, she opened her deep-blue eyes, and though the breeze was cool, it balanced out the warmth from the sun's heat.

A long dock stretched out from the boardwalk, quite a ways into the cove to accommodate the rising tide. She followed it with her eyes, and trailed it to something lying in its center. It was black, but there was a reflection of sorts, and it looked as though it was moving. Paige squinted, trying to get a better view of it, but it was no use. The reflection hid the details of the object too much to make out any details.

"Paige!" The shrill voice of her mother broke her concentration. Her chest instantly tightened with anxiety.

"I'm coming!" Paige yelled back. She took one last look out toward the cove, then scurried back down to the main floor where once again, her parent's eyes were glued to their screens.

"Good. You're back." Cole didn't even look up at his daughter.

Paige looked at the realtor, mouthing her apologies for her rude parents, then caught a glimpse of the closed curtains.

"The view from upstairs was amazing. I'm sure the view from down here is just as good." Paige scampered over to the curtains.

"It is. But it might be a little too bright right now to do the view justice." Ashley did her best to deter the teen from opening them, but it was too late. Light poured into the space, giving the room a cheerful warmth that made both parents lower their phones.

"That is a magnificent view. Isn't it, Cole?" Martha walked across the hardwood floors to stand beside her daughter as her heels clicked along the floor.

Cole joined them.

Ashley cleared her throat in a panic. *What if they see it? What if they want to go out there and see what lies on the marshy floor? Not only will I lose the sale, but 'she' could gain the last one that she needs. And with me being the only other person around…I can't be sure that she'll spare me.*

"Yes. Um…"

Cole and Martha turned around, making eye contact with Ashely for probably the first time since they had been there.

Ashley continued, "The tide goes in and out, so depending on the time of day, you can take a refreshing swim, or go for a walk on the beach."

Paige hadn't turned around. She was searching for the reflection she had seen from upstairs. "I thought I saw something in the middle of the beach. But I can't see it now."

"Oh, Paige, don't be ridiculous. Water from the ocean pours into this cove; it could be anything from a shell to a beer bottle that someone tossed over while on the boat." Martha shook her head and pulled her phone back up.

Ashley relaxed her shoulders. They may be rude, but they covered when it counted. "So, would you like to put an offer in?"

"Yes. We'll take it." Cole shook Ashley's hand then headed out the front door. "Feel free to email us with the details. Martha. Paige. Let's go."

Martha blindly followed.

Paige lingered just a bit then chased after her parents, looking over her shoulder and shouted, "Thank you," to Ashley.

Paige's time off from school for spring beak followed suit with the Simms family moving into their new home in Newburyport, Massachusetts. With only a couple of months left in the school year, Paige knew as a new kid that this would garner the attention she always tried to avoid. *Thanks, Mom and Dad. Perfect timing, as per usual.*

The first couple of days in the house were busy with all forms of chaos, unnecessary yelling and bickering, and a ton of cleaning and organizing. Paige was given the garret as her bedroom which had one of the full bathrooms attached. She had become so focused on getting her room just right that she had forgotten about the door she found during the initial visit.

Martha and Cole took the master bedroom suite on the main level and used the other two bedrooms as their respective offices. True to form, both of them spent the majority of their time at home in said offices, leaving Paige to herself...as usual.

By the weekend, Paige had more or less settled into her new space and once again noticed the door, causing her to remember the deck with a view and ebb and flow of the tide. After breakfast, she grabbed the oversized, wicker chair from the cellar which was rarely used and decided she could make better use of it in her new special space. She took that, some overly stuffed pillows, and a comfy throw blanket up and added her second nightstand. Now she could read, eat, or simply enjoy the salty air away from her parents—the perfect escape.

After taking a look at her new spot, she smiled to herself as she huffed a sigh of satisfaction, and decided to stay up there, snuggle into her comfy chair, and read her current thriller.

Paige squinted as she opened her eyes. *I must have fallen asleep.* The sun was positioned just on the other side of her, which indicated she had slept past noon. Her stomach grumbled. The muffin and banana from breakfast no longer held off her hunger. She bookmarked her page and slid it into her nightstand drawer. Paige then sat on the railing and spun herself down the spiral staircase.

Both parents were hiding in their opposing rooms. Paige made herself a peanut butter and jelly sandwich, sliced up some apples, and grabbed a bag of chips from the pantry. There was no point in telling her parents she'd be outside, so she took a bite of her sandwich and exited the house through the back sliding doors.

Their house was raised on a small hill, which, in hindsight, was good thinking as high tide did tend to get pretty close to the edge of the grassy yard. Paige sauntered down to the yard's edge then debated whether to simply jump down onto the moist sand or take the dock to the edge then jump down. She took another sloppy bite of her sandwich as some of the jelly plopped onto the grass.

Not wanting to risk falling and because the jelly was making a sticky mess of her hands and clothes, Paige decided that she would sit on the edge until she finished eating, then take the dock route to explore more of the wetlands. As she dangled her feet and ate, she watched little creatures dig their way in and out of the sand.

Paige finished her sandwich. She brought her apple to her lips and as she crunched down, the breeze brought a whispering voice, sending a chill through Paige's body. She just about dropped the apple from her mouth. "What the…?"

"Follow the footprints."

"What footprints?"

Starting just before her, footprints sunk into the wet sand, taking just a few steps then they stopped as if waiting for Paige to follow.

Paige put her apple down on her unopened bag of chips then scooted off the dock. Careful not to step directly into the footprints, she followed the growing trail. She looked back every couple seconds, partly out of fear of getting in trouble, and partly hoping that no one would notice. Even though this was beyond her comprehension, it was a fantastic distraction from her mundane, invisible existence in her own family.

Finally, when she got to the center of the cove, the footprints not only stopped moving forward, but they disappeared as well. Paige looked in front of her and saw a black board with white numbers at the top and letters underneath. On either side there was a "yes" and "no".

The sand beside the board cracked and peaked up like an egg shell when a chick wishes to free itself. The object that emerged was a rounded triangle with a slight divot between the closest two points. In the center was a mounded, globe-like dome.

Upon closer inspection, shades of reds, purples, blues and greens swirled behind the glass.

"My collection of souls. They each have their own color."

Paige looked around, trying to find the voice. She was sure nothing good could come from a ouija board anchored to the bottom of the ocean, and yet the voice had such a seductive, inviting tone.

"Aren't they pretty?"

"Why are you collecting them?"

"For someone who just absently followed footprints on her own and found a collection of souls, you don't seem too scared."

"Should I be?"

"Well, given that I need one more soul to escape my cursed entrapment, and you are only one of three living people who has left my old house, I'd say you should be."

"Oh. In that case…maybe there is something we could work out."

"You are a curious one. What is your name?"

"Paige. What's yours?"

"Cordelia Moss."

"Okay, well, Cordelia, from what I gather, you are a sea witch who was cursed to be trapped in this ouija board planchette, and you need souls—"

"Thirteen of them to be precise."

"Right, thirteen souls in order for you to be released into this world. If my calculations are correct, you have twelve now. Do I have it right so far?"

The planchette moved and hovered over the "yes".

"Cute trick."

"Thanks."

"What do you plan on doing once you are freed?"

"So many delicious things. Have a pizza, help clean the oceans, toss some storms around here and there…just to name a few."

"Help clean the oceans? Seriously?"

"Yes. The amount of trash you humans pour into these waters is an absolute crime."

"Don't get me wrong. I agree. You just don't seem like the 'helping humanity' type."

"I did mention storms."

"True. You did. So, how about this? I can give you a soul if you can promise that you'll leave my parents alone. They don't seem to notice me much—that much is obvious since I am talking to you. However, I'm not quite ready to be on my own yet."

"Who do you have in mind?"

"Ashley…the realtor. She kind of forgot to mention this whole thing."

"Yeah. Per my orders. She's been sending me souls for a while now. Not sure I could go back on my agreement with her."

"Okay…though I don't agree. You are a witch, after all."

"Just because I'm a witch doesn't mean I don't have my own moral code. I do have boundaries."

"Fair enough. What soul do you want?"

"Yours looks pretty."

"Fat chance lady." Paige started backing up.

"It'll be fun. It won't hurt much." The planchette wiggled then sprung up into the air like a fish fighting for its life at the end of a hook. It burrowed itself into the sand but Paige could see that it was chasing her. Paige turned and ran, and though she kept telling herself not to look back, she did anyway. It was still in pursuit. She ran faster and passed the dock where she had left her apple and chips. She ran and leaped up onto the grass, tripping and falling over. Paige turned to look, but the planchette, now visible, sat like a sad puppy.

"Until next time, Paige," the wind whispered.

"There won't be a mother-fucking next time." Paige pushed herself up the hill a little farther until she hit its peak then got up and went back to the house.

Not quite used to the new house and all of its quirks yet, the sliding glass storm door was lighter than she was expecting, so it slammed shut behind her. Unfortunately, there had been a crack in the pane, so when it slammed, it shattered, and, to make matters worse, the sound echoed through the house so her parents were now aware.

"Paige! What did you do now?" Both parents stormed out of their offices, but her dad seemed to be taking the lead on this one.

"The wind just blew it shut harder than I meant it to. I can clean it up."

"Damn right you can clean it up. You can also pay for the replacement."

"But I didn't mean to. It was an accident."

"I guess you should be more careful next time."

"So, what, am I supposed to walk on eggshells my whole life? Hoping that I don't do something that is going to upset anyone? You might as well put me in a fucking bubble, if that's the case."

"Watch your mouth, young lady, and just do as you're told." As per usual, Mom just had to put in her pathetic two cents. She never stayed for the execution of it though. Martha pivoted on her heels, which for some stupid reason she still felt the need to wear while indoors, and went back to her office.

"If you want to be in a bubble, you can clean this up then go straight to your room for the rest of the evening. I hope you had a good lunch." Cole threw up his hands and grumbled under his breath then left to his hide-away.

Warm tears of anger swelled up in Pagie's eyes. Her fists were clenched so tight her nails were digging into the palm of her hands and she was shaking.

Instead of grabbing the broom and dustpan, she ran upstairs to her room, slammed her door, then tucked her-self away in the area under the coiled staircase. There wasn't much room in that space, but it was tight enough to feel safe—almost like the room was hugging her…a novelty in the Simms family. Paige pulled her knees into her chest and squeezed them tight as she lay her forehead on her knees, and the tears fell onto her skin.

After a few minutes of sobbing, she wiped her tears from her face, telling herself that it wasn't worth it. She knew she was better than what her parents felt and told her. Paige stood up with a sense of purpose. Her stance was unwavering, until one of the belt loops from her shorts caught on something on the wall. The light from the widow's walk's trap door gave her enough light to see that it was a small hook. While fiddling with the snag, a crack formed in the wall, and a drawer popped out.

After freeing herself, she turned her focus to the drawer. Grabbing the hook, she pulled it towards her. Inside sat a collection of tiny, but perfectly preserved shells, a few pearls, and a geode of sorts. As Paige carefully removed each of the delicate items, she noticed a small journal. It appeared to be black, but as she took it out, she squinted at it for closer scrutiny. She raised it into the light for closer inspection and realized it was a dark, forest green with gold embellishments, one of which was a pentacle.

A frayed once golden, now brownish ribbon marked a place within the journal's pages. Paige slid the bookmark up slightly, enough for her to put a finger in, and opened the book. As she flipped through, she saw recipes that called for things like blood of a rabbit, salt, and sage. Below these entries were verses.

She flipped to the front of the book. "This book belongs to: Cordelia Dawn Moss 1691". Paige looked up at the sky light, then ran up the stairs. The tide had begun to come in, covering the beach and the ouija board. Paige couldn't believe she had found the personal journal of the witch whom she had just met…and almost perished in the process.

Something in her gut bubbled. A fire began to burn with determination—not just to prove to her parents that she was more than a burden—a child that wasn't really wanted—but to help those twelve souls who hadn't been as lucky as Paige…those who were now trapped and not at peace.

"There has to be a way to free them." Paige sat in her chair and started at the beginning of the book, hoping to find something…anything that could help her.

The sun was disappearing, and so was her light, but finally, the last entry of the book held a spell entitled, "Trapping and Freeing of Lost Souls." There was a journal entry next to it.

> *"The village is starting to get weird. The church is investigating all the houses for suspicious works of the devil. I am no work of the devil. I am the work of nature, of truth, and of a power so unique, the devil himself should cower. However, if my intentions are to live a fantastical life, I must find a way to preserve myself. Therefore, I have devised a containment for myself…*
>
> *Anchor me to the earth,*
> *protect me with water,*
> *Let me be heard through wind,*
> *and may my soul burn of fire.*
> *Preserve my being within this sphere,*
> *until I may capture the Thirteenth tear.*
> *For only then can I arrive,*
> *stronger than ever; I will survive.*

"This must be how Cordelia ended up in the planchette. She trapped herself." Paige gazed out once more. The sky glowed in pinks and orange, making water-colors on the rippling tide.

She turned the page but couldn't see the writing. After going back into her room with the light, she still couldn't see it. The writing was too faded.

Paige plopped on the bed and puffed out a breath of frustration. "I have to free them." She rolled over on her side, turning page by page. All of these recipes, these spells, had to have come from somewhere. Unless...at the bottom of each spell, Paige discovered the initials "C.D.M.".

"She wrote them herself!" Paige sprung to her feet and dashed to her desk. She grabbed a pen and paper and began to write.

> *"Free the souls trapped inside,*
> *grant them peace they were denied.*
> *May this curse of thirteen be severed,*
> *for by a witch, they have been tethered."*

Pacing the width of her bed, Paige mumbled the words to ensure she didn't forget and also to make sure that it rhymed. She ripped out the paper, folded it, and tucked it into her bra.

She hesitated with her hand hovering mere centimeters from the door knob to go out to the water's edge. *Was this even going to work, or was it a suicide mission? What if I get caught? What if I don't even make it to the water?* And above all, she wondered, *What if my incantation doesn't even work, it's not like I'm a witch, afterall.*

Paige had to reassure herself that this was the best thing to do, not only for the souls, but to prove herself worthy enough to be a part of the Simms family. No matter the cost....

She opened the door just enough to peek to see if anyone was around. Then she quickly pushed the door open.

Paige had learned early on that opening the door faster was actually less noticeable than a slow, steady creak. Tiptoeing and constantly scouring her surroundings for her parents, she made her way down the steps, across the hall where both parents were in their offices, and to the kitchen.

Forgetting she hadn't cleaned up the glass from before, she stepped on a stray shard. She cupped her mouth to sniffle the groans of pain and profanities and hobbled to the sliding door to escape the house.

Paige crouched down, ensuring her mission was not compromised by her parents, and ran down the slight, grassy hill to the edge of the beach, but with high tide, the beach was only about six inches away. The rest of the area had been covered by water. She took out the paper and recited the spell once more to herself while looking at it and once more with her eyes closed.

Paige, stripped down to her underclothing, slipped her shoes off, then tossed the paper into the air and charged through the chilly water.

"We meet again," the wind said. Paige could picture a most sinister, cocky smile on Cordelia's face…you know…if she had one.

"Better believe it, Bitch. But it's on my terms."

A giggle danced off the breeze past Paige's ear.

Paige finished swimming out to the center of the cove. She gulped in as much air as she could then dove her head below, pushing the water up with her cupped hands as she swam closer to the dark piece of wood. She spotted the planchette, kicked her legs faster, and finally scooped it up with a handful of sand. Paige tilted her body then pushed off the board with her feet, thrusting her up to the surface.

About half way up, a giggle bubbled next to her. A jolt of force yanked her back down to the sand. The urge to breathe was at the forefront of her mind. She yanked and kicked as hard as she could, but the trapped sea witch's power pulled her down like an anchor. There was nothing she could do to save herself except to let go, but letting go would bring doom to the lost souls and dying would grant Cordelia her final soul…she'd be free.

There was only one thing she could do—use her final breaths to free those lost souls and grant them peace. Paige stopped resisting Cordelia's force. Instead, she began to recite…underwater, "Free the souls trapped inside, grant them peace they were denied…" Paige coughed bubbles. Her sight was beginning to blur and darken, but she continued to fight. "May this curse of thirteen be severed, for by a witch, they have been tethered."

Her last few words hurt, her chest felt as she'd imagine the process of making a raisin out of a grape—the life, literally, being drawn out of her.

Screams were the last things Paige heard as her body thumped on the sandy floor, causing the sand to slowly billow around her. She saw swirls of purples, teals, blues, and greens zooming up towards the surface. Then everything went dark.

Everything was still dark, but Paige could feel herself floating back towards the surface. *Am I dead?* She didn't want to open her eyes, but she knew she had to in order to find out if she had succeeded in freeing the souls. Scrunching up her face, Paige opened her eyes. The sliver of the moon looked to be almost smiling at her. She felt warm, confident, and worry-free.

Before heading back to shore, she wanted to see if the ouija board was gone. She dove back down, and to her great relief, the board and the planchette were no longer in sight. The memory of the brilliantly glowing souls flying to their freedom secured Paige's inkling that she had indeed saved them and defeated Cordelia.

Pulling herself up onto the dock, sopping wet, she headed back toward home, where she could hear the typical shouting. This time, however, Cole and Martha were shouting for Paige. A hint of worry echoed in the name. Paige ran to find her parents outside in their immediate backyard.

Though both parents gave a sigh of relief when Cole's flashlight found her, Martha simply couldn't help herself. "Paige Ann Simms, where on Earth have you been?"

"And why in the hell are you soaked? We have been looking for you for half an hour, young lady. You seem to have forgotten that we explicitly told you to clean up the mess of glass you made and you were to stay in your room for the rest of the evening. Honestly, it isn't that hard of a task." Cole shook his head but didn't linger. He turned, removing the light from Paige's face, and began the walk inside.

True to form, Martha followed suit, with both the disapproving head shake and the abandonment.

The anger that boiled within her earlier that day boiled over. Paige could feel every inch of her skin burning with rage. This time, as she clenched her fists, the hairs on her arms and back of her neck stood straight up.

A rumbling of the Earth forced her parents to stop and spin around, both of their flashlights aimed at their daughter. That's when they saw it.

Paige's eyes were a deep, but bold, emerald green, flakes of purple reflected back into Cole's and Martha's faces. Their daughter was hovering mere inches off the grass with a wall of the roaring sea water at her back. Waves crashed forward with the natural ebb and flow of the tide.

"Paige?" Martha shouted.

Paige's head turned in her direction. She blinked a few times, almost as if they were processing what was happening. She looked down, and her body listened, floating gently back down to the grassy yard. While unclenching her fists, the water wall, which had splashed everything within a ten-foot radius, came down and her eyes dulled back to their natural hazel color.

After looking at both of her parents with little concern, she walked between them and back through the slider. Paige casually went to the pantry, grabbed the dustpan and hand broom, and cleaned up her mess. Her parents, in the door frame, silently watched her.

Paige returned everything to its proper place, then turned to her parents, "Good night."

Cole and Martha managed a stiff wave, then they watched their daughter go up to her room.

Paige sat on her chair outside on her secret deck, watching the moon's light skip on the ripples of high tide.

"You released me, you know? I was a trapped soul myself, and you released me."

"I know." Paige closed her eyes and inhaled the pure salty air.

"I think we can do great things together. Don't you?"

"Most definitely." Paige's eyes shot open, the emerald and purple visible once again. And a grin…a grin of triumph.

THE THIRTEENTH ANNIVERSARY

The bathroom was filled with steam. The mirror was completely covered in a thick fog. Katie was sitting in the bathtub as the hot water pulsated onto her back. She watched as the water droplets fell into each other on the shower door then finally dispersed at the bottom. Though the sound, similar to rain, was soothing, it reminded her of her Sam…

Katie and her husband, Sam, had met in the rain. Sam had been an avid runner, while Katie simply liked to read outside at the park on the bench facing the little pond. It was a beautiful day—the sun was out, not many clouds, and there was a faint breeze that prevented the air from getting too stagnant. All of a sudden, the sky got dark in one little spot of the park and rain poured out of the clouds.

In a panic, Katie stood up while putting the book over her head to use as an umbrella, but her hands slipped on the cover and it fell to the ground. When she bent down to get it, her rear end got bumped by a passerby and they both toppled over onto each other.

"I am so sorry. Are you alright?" Sam looked down at Katie with his deep blue eyes and raindrops falling off his nose onto hers.

Katie smiled with squinty 'rain-face' eyes. "I'm fine. But, I'd like to get my book if you don't mind."

"Oh." He realized the slightly awkward position that they were in. "Oh. Of course. Sorry…again." He backed himself off of her to stand. Instead of offering to help her up, he backed up out of her way, towards her book.

Katie rolled herself over to a kneeling position then stood, and without looking up started to move towards her book, and in the process, headbutted Sam, who ended up dropping the book which he had just recovered for her.

They both giggled and rubbed their heads.

"Please, let me. It's the very least I can do." He held up his hand just inches away from her breast, bent over and retrieved her book. "*Behind the Lens* by Kari Holloway, huh?"

"Yea. A little southern romance always brings me a smile."

"Well, in that case," he said, then cleared his throat. With a bow and a lift of the invisible hat off his head, he continued in a deeper southern accent, "My apologies, Ma'am, for my interrupting your reading."

Against the doom and gloom that hovered above their heads, Katie's cheeks blushed a fresh pink.

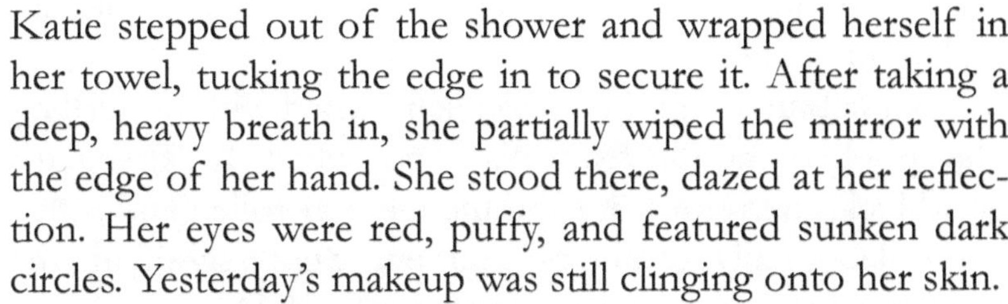

Katie stepped out of the shower and wrapped herself in her towel, tucking the edge in to secure it. After taking a deep, heavy breath in, she partially wiped the mirror with the edge of her hand. She stood there, dazed at her reflection. Her eyes were red, puffy, and featured sunken dark circles. Yesterday's makeup was still clinging onto her skin.

Her hair looked like a bird's nest that got caught up in a terrible storm, but she lacked the motivation to do anything about it.

Katie walked to her bedroom to get dressed and released the towel from her body, letting it drop to the floor of her bedroom. She walked into her closet, but nothing really stood out, except one special T-shirt.…

It was Katie's twentieth birthday. For her party, Sam had put together a surprise for her. An epic battle of Dungeons and Dragons with all of their fantastically nerdy friends. They all wore shirts Sam had printed with the twenty side of an icosahedron die showing. On the top it said, 'Naturally', because, of course, Katie was now twenty, naturally.

The battle had everything you could imagine in it—trolls, gelatinous cube of death, and at the end was the damsel in distress. It was now up to the ranger to defeat the dragon guarding her tower with the help of his fellows and save her.

Sam got down on one knee and asked, "My fair lady, will you do me the honor of marrying me?"

Katie laughed, thinking it was just part of the campaign, but when Sam got a sweaty look at her lack of response, she knew he was serious. She stood up on the verge of tears of joy and opened her mouth to answer, but Sam pulled out a die.

Katie blushed and her stomach turned with butterflies. She grabbed the die from his hand, which he kissed for good luck, then threw it onto the table. It rolled and rolled and rolled, finally landing on a natural twenty, signifying the best possible outcome to any player of D&D.

The whole table jumped up from their chairs, overjoyed for their friends. Katie and Sam kissed to seal the deal, defeated the dragon, and set a wedding date.

Katie wiped a tear from her cheek, grabbed the die T-shirt and the sweatpants she had been wearing ever since he had passed, and curled up under her blankets. Not being able to relax enough to fall asleep—even though she had never remembered a moment when she was more tired than now—Katie rolled over to face his side of the bed. It was empty, yet the impression of his head still lingered on the pillow. She closed her eyes tight and flashed back to that day....

It had been almost a week since Katie had received a call from the hospital. Sam had been rushed into the emergency room. He had been found by the pond where he ran, on the ground and unconscious. They said his breathing was erratic.

Katie rushed over to the hospital as soon as she could, but it was too late. He had already passed. The doctor told her that they hooked him up to an EKG in the ambulance and noticed an arrhythmia. Ventricular fibrillation.

"Did he ever mention anything about a murmur?"

"No. Never. He ran for his whole life. Never had any problems, except for running into people." She started to laugh but the heaviness of the situation hit her like a ton of bricks, and the laughter quickly turned to uncontrollable sobbing. In bearable coherent mumbles, she told the doctors, "It is our thirteenth anniversary in…" she had to count, "thirteen days. I just, I don't understand."

"I'm so very sorry for your loss, Mrs. Morris." The doctors left her to her grief.

"And here we are. One week until our anniversary. The year of the moonstone." Katie was talking to the pillow where his head would be. "I got you something…had it all ready for you."

She scrambled out of bed, back into the closet and tossed anything out of her closet that was in the way of her getting his gift. She grabbed a box from behind her dresses and sat back on the bed with it. Inside the box was a small, black satchel with gold thread outlining the moon. Katie opened it and dumped out the set of Dungeons and Dragons moonstone dice. Having picked up the icosahedron, she found the twentieth side and rubbed the number with her thumb.

"You were always better at gift giving than I was. I know you had something already too. Care to share?" She chuckled as tears steadily streamed down her face. Katie, almost in anger, got out of bed and began to rummage through Sam's side of the bedroom, catching a glimpse of the full moon outside their bedroom window; she could have sworn she saw a shooting star. "I wish I was with you, Sammy." In her grief-ridden adrenaline, she collapsed to her knees then onto her side. "Why?" she screamed. Her voice cracked with heartbreak. Her eyes shut tight and every muscle in her body tensed. "Why did you leave me?"

The tears continued for a few minutes, though it felt like hours had gone by. Her body had gone numb and her tears had dried. Katie opened her eyes. She was looking into the abyss under their bed. It was dark, but the light from behind the headboard revealed something in the corner that wasn't usually there.

Katie, a bit shaky, inched a little closer then reached under the bed and toward the object. It was a precious, quaint, gray box, tied with a beautiful, purple ribbon, her favorite color.

Katie took her time untying the ribbon's bow. When she opened the box, a beautiful moonstone ring reflected the little light it was catching—a silver braided band that hugged a teardrop moonstone.

"Oh, Sam. It's absolutely magical."

As she went to take it out of the box, she noticed a corner of paper sticking out from the side of the platform where the ring was nestled. Katie removed the platform to discover a note, handwritten by Sam. It read:

> *I'm sorry I never told you. I wanted us to live a life free from the fear of death. But the reaper was knocking on the door. I'm proud of the life we shared and look forward to our next...*
>
> *Wish upon the brightest moon*
> *While wearing this precious token*

And together we will be soon
Once these words have been spoken
-Sam

Katie placed it upon her finger, opposite her wedding band. After getting off the floor, she gently kissed Sam's pillow, walked around the bed, and turned off her light. While staring at the moon, her body was able to relax, her racing heartbeat had slowed to a more regular pace, her eyes finally felt heavy enough to close, and she drifted off, mumbling the words Sam had written, and thinking how nice it would be…

THE THIRTEENTH FLOOR

A crowd swarmed together, mumbling and pointing up to the man on the ledge of the thirteenth floor of an office building. The man's name was Aaron Donaldson. He had quite the reputation for being a cut-throat lawyer, defending the slime at the very bottom of society's bucket. Despite his undesirable clientele, everyone still referred to him as a highly confident and competent lawyer and man. So, when his friend, Peter Williams, came onto the scene, he was utterly confused.

"What the hell, Aaron?" Peter kept looking up at his friend while pushing through the crowd. *Maybe I can get to him.* He finally forced his way through and ran into the building. Peter pressed the elevator button, hoping it would be waiting for him, but it seemed to be stuck at the thirteenth floor. Running for the stairs, Peter skipped over every other step to get to Aaron as soon as possible.

Finally, he reached the access door to the thirteenth floor, their company's workspace. Peter saw Aaron standing on the ledge, broken glass everywhere around him. Peter didn't want to spook his friend, but he didn't want to be too late either.

"Aaron? Um…Whatcha doin', bud?"

Aaron didn't acknowledge.

Peter weaved through the glass. As he drew closer, he heard Aaron talking to someone, and upon taking a quick gander around the space, Peter saw a dark, fuzzied figure standing next to Aaron whispering in his ear.

Peter ran through the glass, no longer caring if he cut up himself or his high-dollar shoes.

A piercing screech reverberated off the walls, forcing Peter to his knees, and when there was a pause in the hellish sound, he looked up to see the shadowed figure standing all too close to him. Its face was terribly morphed with hollow eyes and dark sunken circles. It had snake-like slits for a nose, and the mouth was sewn shut, and yet it spoke. Then, it smiled…a sickly-evil grin. It opened its mouth, the threads unraveling and fraying as it did, then with another piercing shriek, more windows broke, and Aaron jumped.

Peter rushed to the ledge. *Maybe he caught something and there is still a chance. Maybe the people below caught him.* But there was no saving his friend, for when Peter looked down, there was a mutilated body below, the crowd had moved out of the way and now formed a spectator's circle around him. Even though Peter knew Aaron was dead on impact, he still rushed down to be by his side.

Peter held his friend's hand, waiting for the ambulance to arrive. When they took Aaron away, daunted by the distance he had fallen, Peter looked up where his friend last stood. There. The shadowed figure stared back at him. It looked as if it even blew him a kiss. A split second later,

Peter felt a fog—a dizziness and hatred towards himself that he only divulged in while drinking his worries away. Bringing his hand up to his head to brace himself, he noticed a mark on his palm.

The shape of the mark was distinct, but it was one he hadn't ever seen before. An 'M' sat on a line, but an 'X' could be seen as well, the center being the base of the middle of the 'M'. Peter had no idea what this meant, but he was sure the kiss from the creature that had just forced his friend to commit suicide by jumping off the cursed thirteenth floor had something to do with it…and it was not a good thing.

The scene was closed down for the rest of the day. And given the fact Aaron's death was the third occurance in the same way in a month, the partners of the company decided to relocate for the time being to the sixteenth floor while the proper authorities could investigate.

Peter walked home. It was a long walk, but he had a lot to think about and knew that if he went right home, there would be distractions—like television—to keep his mind off the very real possibility that he was next…the next to die.

Peter didn't sleep much in the following week, but everyone in the company was due back at the office building as the move to the sixteenth floor was finalized. The mark on his hand hadn't bothered him much other than not knowing the full details of having such a mark. Quite frankly, he was eager to go back to work. Working from home was distracting. He felt trapped within his own thoughts - the scene of that day replaying in his mind in addition to the constant questions of this mark. Being back in the office, he felt, would help him get out of his head and focus on other things like the water cooler gossip or watching Ashley toy around with the boss.

He walked into the building and pressed the up-elevator button. He was the only one to board, as he was earlier than normal. Out of habit, Peter pressed the thirteenth button, then quickly pressed sixteen—not that it would void the thirteen, even though he secretly hoped it would magically go dim, but he did still have to get to the new floor.

As expected, the doors opened on the thirteenth floor. It was a skeleton floor at this point. Other than the cubicle walls that once divided busy workers and the remnants of loose paper, there was nothing left but the bones of the building itself, the yellow caution tape, and boarded up windows. A pile of glass gathered in the center of the open space from all the shattered windows—a reminder of the weeks before. The media had no ideas on how that had happened, but Peter knew all too well.

"Peter." A shrill voice whispered, blowing an eerily cool breeze through the building. A vision of the figure popped in his head. He repeatedly jammed his thumb for the sixteenth floor, thinking the faster he pressed the button the sooner the doors would close.

Only a sliver of an opening left, and there it was—the demon's face peeking in. "Peter," it said again with a grotesque grin. It reached its long vaporish fingers through the gap, then it disappeared when the doors sealed shut. The elevator jolted upwards. Had Peter just escaped death?

Peter was sure to not mistake the elevator button again for the rest of the week. But as the week did go on, his hand with the mark became more agitated. It was hot when he was in the building, then it was itchy while he was home and it had cooled off—as if it were trying to heal—but every day in the building, it would reaffirm its place on his hand.

By Wednesday, the palm of his hand was inflamed and a spot had opened due to the constant scratching he did in the middle of the night.

He wrapped his hand up before going into work on Thursday. He could swear it was infected at this point. The edges of his skin that had been marked seemed seared…tinged with black. It was raw, sore, and hot to the touch. By the time he left that day, he felt as though he might be running a fever. He got into the elevator, the cluster of his associates joining him, all heading to the main floor.

The elevator went down smoothly as per usual until the fourteenth floor. The cables cried and the elevator box pulled up and down, like playing tug-of-war with itself. The chime rang for the thirteenth floor. Banging noises made everyone jump. The doors were trying to open by themselves but finally the forces at play lost the fight. The doors sealed shut and the elevator box almost dropped to make up for lost time. Finally, the doors opened on the main floor. Everyone flew out in relief. Some were saying they wouldn't be using the elevator for a while.

By the time Friday came around, Peter felt like death itself…or maybe that would be a relief. He was late this time, given his current feverish condition, but he was damned if he was going to stay home again to be lost in his thoughts. Work was the only escape.

He shuffled into the elevator by himself. Giving a sloppy attempt to fix his appearance, he jostled his tie, tightened, then straightened it. Afterwards, discovering his shoelace had become untied, he kneeled over as the elevator began its ascent to the sixteenth floor.

The air began to choke him. He stood, gasping for breath. His shirt was drenched with sweat, and his brow also dripped in the excess of it. The elevator's alarm rang out and buzzed then came to a staggering halt. Closing his eyes as the air strangled him more and more, Peter had no choice but to pry the doors open to get some fresh air.

The thirteenth floor.

There it was. The demon figure standing in the distance across the room. Long, shadowy talons stretched out and gripped around Peter's neck, pulling him out of the elevator. The doors slammed shut, and a massive crash bellowed with drywall smoke as the elevator's cables snapped and dropped to the basement storage floor of the building.

The demon's opaque white eyes seared with a black, tinged fire circling around and around.

"Peter." The mouth parted again, just like it had when Peter tried to save Aaron. The fraying strings curled up like lighting a candle's wick, all to fray again and continue the cycle.

Completely at a loss of what to do, Peter was forced to relive the day he had let his friend jump. The overwhelming guilt of such a precious loss gutted Peter. His thoughts took over, and in turn, allowed the demon deeper into his mind.

Suddenly, Peter could breathe again. He ignored the crushing of glass underneath his shoes, the piercing pain of a shard cutting through his foot as it punctured his flesh, and walked to the window's edge.

It didn't look so high this time…nothing but a jump into a lake…a lake that swirled with the lost souls of those before him.

Almost as if accepting his fate, Peter lifted a foot into the air outside the building.

"Don't," the faintest whisper hung in the breeze. It sounded like Aaron, but Peter knew it couldn't be, for he had watched him fall…hadn't he?

He turned—not only to double check his hearing, but also to decide if there was a better chance for him to follow through if he didn't see the pavement down below—and saw that the demon no longer wore his own face, but rather the face of Aaron.

The demon's smile stretched so much so that Aaron's face began to peel away, once again revealing its true self.

"Peter. Jump."

The Thirteenth Headstone

There was a knock at the door. As soon as Melissa's parents answered it, the two tornadoes named Liam and Declan bulldozed their way in, in search of the third musketeer, Melissa's little brother, Adam.

"Amy. Jon." Maura kissed Melissa's parents on the cheek.

"Come on in. I just have to finish getting ready, and Tom is just writing all the numbers down for the girls."

Stacy, Melissa's friend and co-babysitter for the night, came in after her parents, slipped off her shoes, and headed for Melissa's room.

"Hey." Stacy popped her head in the room. "Ready for tonight?"

"Eh. I don't mind babysitting, really. But those three boys are nuts."

Stacy laughed. "At least we get to babysit together for a change. It was genius to propose a double date to the parents. This way, we get to gang up on them instead of the reverse."

"Totally."

"So, what is the plan for the night?"

"I don't know. Adam was last seen in the tree house. I have a feeling we'll be outside for most of the time."

"Girls. Come on down, please. We are getting ready to leave," Tom called from the kitchen.

"Coming," Melissa shouted back.

"Now girls, we wrote down the number to the restaurant where we'll be, emergency numbers, of course, and here is money and the number for pizza." Melissa's mom handed Melissa the money and the piece of paper with the numbers on it. "I just checked on the boys. They are outside in their treehouse with their flashlights."

"Sounds like a spooky night of ghost stories." Jon chuckled with a wink.

"Maybe so. But, girls, remember, they are only nine and you know how Declan can get. Don't scare them too much." Amy nudged her husband for the encouragement of easing up on any such torment.

"I promise, Mom. Have a good night." Stacy hugged her parents, then both girls walked all parents to the door.

"Call us if you need anything," Maura said as her husband all but dragged her out the door.

"We'll be fine, Mom," Stacy assured.

Both parties waved good-bye as the parents pulled out of the driveway in Tom's blue and brown Vista Cruiser.

Once the car had turned the corner, the girls walked back inside and ordered the pizza before checking on the boys, who had already started with the stories.

Adam was standing up, and even though he was the same age as the twins, he towered over them in his pose—his back slightly hunched, arms above his head with claws for hands, and stomped toward Declan and Liam.

"The bear smelled the…" He looked at the package the twins were eating from. "He smelled the 'Ding Dongs' and tore his way through the tent, snatched the box right out of the kid's hand, then…"

The twins' eyes widened in anticipation.

"Sat on the kid and ate the rest of the box."

Declan and Liam looked at each other, then busted out laughing.

"That's not scary at all."

"Yeah, that wasn't scary," Declan copied his brother.

"Admit it. I had you going for a while though, right?"

The boys just shook their heads.

Adam plopped on the floor across from them and lunged for the box, but the twins defended their treats. "Then you tell one."

Declan looked at Liam. "How about the one about the lake monster?"

Liam scrunched his face. "Everyone knows that one. What about…" He tapped his chin with his pointer finger.

"The nameless headstone!" Melissa popped her head through the treehouse's entrance.

Melissa and Stacy had quietly sneaked up the ladder to the treehouse and had been eavesdropping.

Adam jumped up and struck a ninja pose. Declan rolled over into the corner, and Liam just threw a 'Ding Dong' at Melissa's face as she pulled herself up.

The girls were cracking up to the point of tears as they both climbed in and found a spot in the corner on the pillows and blankets.

Once the boys' hearts slowed to a normal pace, they sat back in their circle but opened it up to include the girls.

"So, do you boys think you can handle such a tale?" Stacy looked at her brothers. They were so different from one another for being identical twins. Liam just shrugged his shoulders. Declan lowered his gaze. "If you get scared, you can come sit on my lap." Declan nodded.

"Adam, you game? You can always attack with your ninja skills and save us all if something bad were to happen." Melissa bit her lips shut, covering up her urge to laugh.

"Ha, ha. Very funny. We already know this story though. Dad tells us every Halloween."

"Why on Halloween? It has nothing to do with that." Liam furrowed his eyebrows.

"Um, it has everything to do with Halloween."

"Okay…interesting…sounds like we may have a couple variations here. How about Liam and I tell our family's version, and you and Adam can tell yours?" Stacy looked at Melissa with a feisty type of grin.

"Deal." Adam readjusted in his spot. "But I want to go first."

"No way. It was Stacy's idea, so we should go first."

"Yeah, we should go first."

Both twins and Stacy scowled at Adam.

"Fine. But I get a 'Ding Dong'."

At first the twins hugged the box, but Stacy gave them a look, easily persuading Declan to toss one to Adam.

"Ok. It was a stormy night. The waves on the shore were higher than the Statue of Liberty."

"Bullshit." Adam interrupted Liam.

"No, it's not." Declan defended his brother.

"Adam. Watch your language and listen. It'll be our turn next."

"Humf." Adam leaned against the wall of the tree-house and crossed his arms.

"As I was saying…" Liam shot a glare at Adam who reciprocated by sticking out his tongue. "The waves on the shore were higher than the Statue of Liberty. The sky was dark except the last sliver of sun on the horizon…the color of blood. Lightning struck on the beach and then again on a tall pole out in the ocean."

Stacy hunkered down. "While all this was going on, some kids, only a year or two older than you guys, were down at the beach, hiding in the tall grasses. Everytime the lighthouse shined its light out into the ocean, they could see a ship with a tattered flag getting closer and closer until…it stopped."

"The crashing of the waves quieted, and the clouds floated away with the light breeze, but the kids could still hear something, and the sound got closer and closer— footsteps from the water to the sand. A brave kid…"

"Billy."

"I'm telling the story, Stacy."

Stacy giggled but sat back and raised her arms in sur-render.

"A brave kid named Billy fumbled for his flashlight when the footsteps stopped. He turned it on and tracked the beach with his eyes, but nothing was in sight. But when he went to stand up, a hand grabbed him on the shoulder."

Declan quickly crawled over to Stacy and curled up on her lap.

Adam rolled his eyes yet scooted closer to Liam to en-sure he didn't miss out on any details.

"The man who had grabbed Billy had a scar across his left eye, his beard was long and matted, and his skin looked as rough as sandpaper. 'Show me where you bury your dead, boy,' the pirate barked in a deep raspy voice. Little

Billy looked around for his friends, but pirates had George and Marshall in their grips as well. Too scared to speak, the three boys pointed in the direction of the chapel with the cemetery.

"Shoving the boys the whole way there, they marched towards the cemetery. They walked down the first row of headstones and stopped at the first empty plot—number thirteen. The main pirate who had Billy looked back towards the shoreline, looking a bit on edge, which made Billy and his friends even more fearful for their lives. After one of the pirates threw down some shovels, the scarred pirate demanded for the boys to, 'Start digging.'"

"Then what happened?" Adam asked with wide eyes.

"Well, the story goes, while the boys were digging, more pirates showed up and attacked the scarred one and his men. In the midst of all the action, Billy, George, and Marshall got out of the grave and ran to the chapel. As dawn approached, Billy and his friends could see the scarred pirate slay the last of the unwelcome 'guests'. He then emptied their pockets and those of his now dead crew, and buried the gold he had stashed away under his coat in the grave. The pirate then looked in the direction of the chapel, tilted his hat with a wink, and left the island…never to return."

"So, did Billy and his friends dig up the treasure?"

"No one knows. Some say Billy and his friends divided up the treasure, buried the dead pirate bodies, and placed a nameless stone on the site."

Adam let out an unfavorable sigh.

"But some say that Billy, George, and Marshall were so thrown by the night's events that they promised each other never to step foot in the cemetery again."

"So it could still be there?"

Melissa and Stacy snickered in the corner with Declan still on Stacy's lap.

"I mean…if your story is even true."

Liam just shook his head.

"I'm going to check to see if the pizza is here yet." Stacy picked Declan off her lap. "Do you want to come with me, or listen to Adam and Melissa's version of the story? I'll only be gone for a moment."

"I can stay. I don't think it could be that scary. Right?" Declan looked over at Adam who had the most sinister grin on his face.

"You can come sit in my lap if you wish." Melissa opened her arms and welcomed him.

Stacy went down the ladder.

Adam readjusted to sit on his knees and feet. "Years ago there were witches among us— evil people who toyed with people's lives—cursing their friends so they would grow ill, forcing people to fall in love…"

All the boys scrunched up their faces, "Blech."

"I know, right. Anyway, they would even kill anyone who dared cross them. There was this one woman named Jocelyn, who was the schoolhouse teacher. All the kids loved her. She would play with the kids at recess, bring in treats, and she didn't even give a lot of homework."

"No way. What teacher doesn't give out homework?" Liam shook his head and rolled his eyes.

"I listened to yours—now it's my turn."

"At least mine was believable."

"Oh, yeah..sure… cuz pirates killing pirates for a little bit of gold and then not even taking it with them is really believable."

Liam and Adam took turns shouting back and forth while Melissa tried to break it up, which was made all the more difficult due to holding Declan, who was covering his ears.

"Liam, Adam…sit down." Stacy had returned with the pizza and some paper plates and napkins. "You told your version of the story, Liam. Now it is Adam's turn. You will sit and listen, just as he did for you."

"Yes, ma'am."

"Now eat some food and shut your pie hole."

Liam stuck out his tongue at his sister but listened nonetheless.

Adam took a huge bite of pizza and continued with a very full mouth, "This teacher, Jocelyn, was loved by all, until a new kid, Tommy Fisher, showed up. He was a real bully. He pushed other kids, took their lunches—even beat up a couple of kids. One day, Jocelyn caught Tommy in the act of bashing this kid's face in. She brought him into the school room and smacked his hands with a ruler."

"I thought you said this teacher was nice." Declan peeked out from his hands that were covering his face.

"Nice to nice children, bad to bad."

Declan nodded in agreement, accepting the explanation.

"Naturally, Tommy didn't appreciate that too much. So that night he went back home and told his parents about this mean teacher. By the time the full moon was shining bright, there was a mob outside of Jocelyn's house chanting, 'Kill the witch, kill the witch.'"

Declan curled up into an even smaller ball on Melissa's lap while she patted the floor helping her brother keep the beat of the anti-witch chant.

"Tommy's father, among others, knocked down the door and dragged her out by her hair. They tied her to a pole and set her aflame. But, by dawn, Jocelyn had not even one burn on her body."

"She was still alive?" Liam's jaw almost looked detached; his shock was evident.

Adam smiled his coy smile and nodded his head ever so slowly. "Not one burn," he repeated for effect. "That was proof to all the townspeople she was, indeed, a witch. They let her down but decided if they couldn't kill her by fire, there was no way of killing her. Instead, they took her to the thirteenth plot in the church cemetery and buried her alive. They say if you go there on a full moon, you can hear her and the snap of her ruler."

"I don't believe that for one second. Even a witch would burn."

Adam stood up. "No she wouldn't. Not all witches are the same. Our story is the right one." Adam looked at his sister to back him up, but she was busy trying to comfort Declan.

Liam stood up and shuffled right next to Adam, then whispered, "There's only one way to find out the truth."

Adam balled up his fists and glanced at the girls, who weren't paying them any attention at this point. "Can you get your parent's keys?"

Liam nodded.

"And some shovels. There's one leaning by the shed. Mom just used it yesterday for gardening."

Liam nodded again.

"Meet you at the car."

First Liam started to climb down, very quietly.

But when it was Adam's turn, Melissa noticed. "Where are you going?"

"Ah…to the bathroom."

"Where did Liam go?"

"Ah…to the bathroom?"

"What are you two up to?" Melissa picked Declan up and placed him on Stacy's lap, then stood up, creeping towards the exit hatch.

Adam jumped down to the grass and darted for the backdoor that Liam had left open. He slid it shut and locked it behind him.

Melissa, now running towards the house, yelled out Adam's name.

Adam closed the front door behind him and got into the car that Amy and Jon had left.

Liam shut the trunk with the shovel in it and got into the driver's seat.

"Hurry, let's go!"

"Have you ever driven before?"

"No, but how hard can it be?" Liam shrugged his shoulders then turned the key and started the engine. After backing out of the driveway, he scraped the passenger side mirror against the mailbox. He looked over at Adam. "I guess it's a little harder than it looks."

Liam shifted gears and squealed the tires as the two boys sped down the road, heading for the chapel and the "haunted" cemetery.

By the time Melissa had gotten over the backyard fence, the boys were turning the corner for Main Street.

"It is pretty dark out here." Adam kind of chuckled.

"That's okay. My dad keeps flashlights in his emergency kit in the trunk."

"That's handy." Adam looked behind them, checking if he could see his sister running after them. "You think they'll catch up?"

"At some point. But what can they do? We'll already be at the cemetery digging."

"True enough."

Liam pulled right up to the cemetery and parked the car so that the lights were pointing at the thirteenth headstone.

Adam was looking around, not getting out of the car.

"Are you going to chicken out on me?"

"Yeah, right…just making sure no one else is out there and wondering if I should kiss the ground now that we've stopped, that's all."

"Haha, very funny. Let's go, chicken shit."

"Yeah, let's go see if there is a live witch or some buried treasure."

"You're so confident and everything, but which would you rather find? Would you rather be right and we die at the hands of a witch, or would you rather be wrong and find gold?"

"I don't want to answer."

Liam belted out a laugh. "You just did."

"Whatever. Let's just do this."

"After you." Liam tossed Adam the shovel from the trunk while he brought the flashlights.

They walked over together. The stone was indeed nameless. In fact, there wasn't any carving in it at all…no dates, no symbols, no epitaph, nothing. It was rather smooth given all the wear and tear from the weather over who knows how long. Even more interesting and strange was that there were beautiful yellow, red, and orange poppies blooming in front of it.

Adam marched over to the grave, gazed up at Liam, who was cracking a smug smile, then plunged the shovel into the soil. After about ten or fifteen minutes, Adam threw the shovel up to Liam. "Your turn."

"You made quite a dent. Is digging some kind of hobby of yours?"

"No. Well, I guess."

Liam picked up the shovel, cocked an eyebrow, and paused, waiting for further explanation.

"Well, it isn't like I make a habit of digging for the dead if that's what you mean. But I do help my mom in the garden on the weekends."

"Oh. Okay." He shrugged then jumped down into the hole and started his shift.

After another ten minutes, Liam tapped out.

"Your poor little arms getting tired, Liam?"

"Oh shut up and dig, mama's boy."

"I'll be a mama's boy. Helping in the garden has obviously given me more muscles. I wonder if Ashley Bowman likes muscles."

"No fair. You know I like her."

"Maybe so. But maybe she likes muscles."

"Well…maybe I'll help my mom in the garden."

"I'd love to see that."

"Laugh all you want, green thumb. Just dig."

Adam kept digging for another couple minutes, when finally, *clink*.

Liam jumped into the hole with Adam. Using their hands, they dug around a decent-sized metal container.

"I told you it was treasure."

"Oh, it's treasure alright." A man's voice surprised them from above. "But not the kind of treasure you are expecting."

"Dad?" Liam flashed his light in the direction of the voice. Sure enough, the whole family was there, and so was Adam's family.

Tom reached down for Adam's hand and helped pull him up. Jon did the same with Liam. Then, to the boy's surprise, both fathers jumped in. They finished digging up the metal box then hoisted it up, handing it to Maura and Amy.

Tom and Jon lifted themselves up out of the plot.

Stacy and Melissa smacked their two brothers on the back of the head, ensuring the parents didn't see; the boys stifled their groans, knowing that they had deserved it.

Both families huddled around the container. Maura brushed off the top of the box.

"I can't believe you boys found this." Amy wiped a tear from her cheek. Declan parted from Stacy and sat in his mom's lap to comfort her.

Adam and Liam shifted their gaze from one parent to the next, and almost simultaneously asked, "What is it?"

"Treasures from the past." Maura sniffled. Tom cupped his hand around his wife's cheek.

"What does that mean?" Liam raised his voice slightly, increasingly getting impatient.

"Yeah, can we open it?" Adam whispered, hoping he wouldn't get in trouble.

Jon nodded. "I'll get the cutters from the trunk."

"There isn't a key?" Declan looked up with curiosity at his mom.

Amy shook her head.

"I'm sure there is. Just not sure where it is at this point. Last I knew, Sheriff Hudson had it," Melissa stated.

"Same, but after his passing last year to cancer…I'm not sure who ended up with it."

Tom laughed. "That son of a gun probably had it buried with him."

"Wouldn't doubt that for one minute," Jon agreed, now back with the cutters. He crouched down and cut the padlock.

Maura and Amy both took in a deep breath, each holding one side of the container, then opened the lid.

All the kids leaned forward to see what treasures lay inside, but leaned back once they saw 'junk'.

"Mom, what is all this stuff?" Melissa reached in the box and pulled out some letters which uncovered trinkets and odds and ends.

"Well, this…," Maura reached in and pulled out a locket. She opened it up and showed it to her daughter. "This is your grandma and your grandfather."

"Your dad? But I thought he was dead."

Melissa shoved her brother.

"What?"

"You are right. Your grandfather did pass. I was only a few months old when your grandfather was drafted into the war. And they didn't know at the time, but they found out a few weeks after he had left that Grandma was pregnant again with your Aunt Samantha, who was named after him, Samuel Lee Fields."

"And these are my father's dog tags." Amy pulled a chain with bloodied tags hanging.

"What about all of these letters?" Melissa held up the letters.

"May I?" Jon reached out for them. "My mother and father wrote to each other as often as possible. I was about five years old when an officer came to the door knocking. There weren't any dog tags or anything. He was missing in action. To this day, they haven't found anything from his squadron. He was a pilot. They assumed that his plane was shot down along with many of his friends."

"The other objects are from other people who lost family during this time. For example, Sheriff Hudson's father was a drunk, but his mom was an army nurse and was killed during her service." Tom pulled out a hat. "This was his mother's nursing hat. He had been staying with his aunt.

After they got the news that his mother had died, his father left for an alcohol run and never returned."

"What is this?" Stacy pulled out a metal pendant attached to a purple ribbon.

"That is a purple heart. Both my grandfather and father were in a war. My grandfather had served in World War II and was awarded the purple heart. He did everything in his power to keep his men safe. He and his men were moving out to a new location, and they were being bombed. He thought everyone had gotten out, but when he did his count, he was short three men. There was a building on fire, which was the only place they hadn't been able to check. He went in and heard shouting and coughing. It was his men. One by one, he helped them out of the building. With the last soldier in his arms, the building started to collapse. His other men were right out the door, helping those my grandfather was saving. My grandfather was close enough to the door to roll his injured men towards the door, all while his leg was pinned under rubble. He thought he wasn't going to make it, but he ensured that all of his men were given the best chance to make it home. Ironically enough, those three men whom he had saved, came back for him. He lost the leg, but he was alive, allowing him to accept the purple heart. Before my father left for Vietnam, his father gave him the purple heart for good luck. Dad came back, but wasn't the same. "

"These stories are amazing. Why would you all tell us ridiculous stories about pirates and schoolhouse witches?" Stacy picked up some pictures that were standing up on the side of the box.

The parents looked at each other. "I don't know for sure. Maybe it was that we wanted to keep the pain away from you all." Amy squeezed the twins and Stacy tight to her.

"Maybe we just wanted to remember them the way they were. Digging this up would be digging up some pretty painful memories for many people." Maura wiped her face and squeezed her husband's arm.

"We should pay tribute to these people," Liam boldly stood up and proclaimed.

"I agree…but I want to add to the time capsule as well." Adam followed suit.

"What do you propose?" Tom lifted his head from the box of treasures, looking at the bright, young boys before him.

Liam walked around to the back of the nameless headstone. "I think we should have the headstone done as a memorial for those that you all remember here—carve all their names in the stone."

"Yeah!" Adam shouted. "We can add the stories that you all told us into the box, but on the outside, the town will all know a bit of their family's history."

Declan stood up from his mom's lap. "You think we could have it done by the Fourth of July?" It was only three weeks away.

"I think that is a grand idea." Maura began to well up in tears again.

On the Fourth of July, after setting up blankets and chairs in the field just past the church, all families involved with the time capsule gathered around the hole in the ground at the cemetery. The mayor unveiled the new headstone which revealed eighteen names of men and women from the community now represented as a tribute. At the top, the stone was engraved: "In memory of those we lost: 1942-1975."

Due to the condition of the previous box, the group decided to get a bigger box for the new time capsule.

"Someone is going to have to dig a bigger hole for this one to fit." Tom side-eyed the boys.

"I'll help dig!" Liam grabbed a shovel.

"I want to dig too." Adam glared at him.

"Lucky for you, I have another shovel you can use." Jon handed Adam a shovel.

"Alright, you boys go ahead and start digging, we are going to get the food set up." Amy kissed Liam on the forehead, which he promptly wiped off when she turned. Everyone else followed. Just Liam and Adam stayed to dig.

"We'll check on you in a bit." Tom tousled Adam's hair then followed.

The boys jumped into the hole and started digging.

Adam wiped his brow then admired the restored headstone, sliding his hand over each name. The poppies that had been there were gone now, uprooted for the restoration, but they would be replanted once the restoration was complete. Now, however, Adam had the chance to see the base of the stone.

"Liam, look at this!"

Liam hopped over.

"Look here. It has her name on it." 'Jocelyn Grey' was carved in the smallest possible print at the base of this ancient gravestone. "I told you the witch was here. Maybe she is buried on the other side?" Adam dropped his shovel and started to climb out of the hole.

"Adam, don't be ridiculous. That could be anybody."

"Anybody with the same name as a witch who supposedly was buried here? That's a pretty big coincidence."

Liam shrugged. "Maybe so, but I'm hungry and don't want to miss the fireworks. Can we just finish this? This witch, if she is there, will still be there on another night when we decide to dig up graves."

They both laughed.

"Fine. Let's keep digging."

Liam went back over to his original spot and continued to dig, and Adam took one last look at the name of a thousand questions.

Liam picked up a scoop of dirt and plopped it down only to notice something shiny in the midst of the grime. He bent down and picked it up. It was a coin, but not one he had ever seen before. It was about the size of a half dollar. Though the back of it was fairly plain in design, the front was stamped with a moline cross and an intricate border. Some of it was worn down, but the boys could tell what it was.

"Adam," Liam whispered. "Take a look at this."

Adam made his way over.

The euphoric glee in both of the boys' eyes radiated.

"The pirates? The witch? Both are true?"

Adam saw another piece of gold shining where Liam had just dug. He picked it up and put it in his pocket as Liam put his piece in his pocket.

"Are there more?"

They dropped to their knees, then using their hands, they felt around for more. One last piece was all they could find.

"What should we do with it?" Liam rolled it in his hands.

"Well, you have one. I have one. What about putting this one in the box?"

"Let's do it! And how about we just keep this between us. Deal?"

"Deal."

The boys spat in their hands, slapped them together, and shook on it.

With the biggest smiles on their faces, Liam and Adam dug a big enough hole for the new "treasure". They called over their families then placed the new letters people had created with the old items. Adam was the last to put his letter in. He slipped in the coin, gave a wink to Liam, then stepped back.

Boom. Boom.

Mr. Jon took the shovel from Adam. "Sounds like the fireworks are starting. You all go watch them. Mr. Tom and I can fill in the hole."

The boys smiled then darted across the field.

"Last one there's a one-legged pirate!"

"Or a burning witch!"

The Thirteenth Key

I watched the trees pass me by as I looked out the bus window. The past few days had been a whirlwind, and I was still trying to wrap my head around it all, reliving the conversation from that pivotal day.

Three days ago, the phone rang.

"My name is Andrew Livingston. Is Brie Covell available?" the voice on the other end asked.

"Speaking."

"I'm afraid I have some bad news. Your grandmother, Madison Newman, has passed away. You are mentioned in her will. Would you be able to meet me at the office this morning?"

"Newman is my mother's maiden name, but I don't have any living grandparents on that side of the family."

"Yes. That is mentioned in the will. However, it appears she knew about you, and it is important you attend."

"Okay." After writing down the address and hanging up the phone, I got myself ready and headed out.

When I got there, I was informed that my grandmother, whom I never knew had existed, had left me her entire estate—a supposed mansion somewhere in Romania. I called my mother after the meeting only for her to once again deny the whole thing, claiming I was being scammed. And yet, I heard a nervous twinge in her voice which only confirmed the information to be true.

Honestly, I'm not sure why I even bothered asking her. After all, I had questioned so many things as a child…all of which were instantly shut down. But it isn't like I could forget the questions since the dreams and blackouts have only increased as I have gotten older.

I decided I wasn't going to take Mother's denial as my answer this time. I needed answers, and if they weren't going to be handed to me, I would have to figure it out for myself. Without telling my parents what I was planning, I booked my flight and packed a bag.

Three days later…here I am. The plane landed early this morning. The only way to get close to where I needed to be was to hail a bus. And, by the looks of it, it had just arrived.

As soon as I got off, I could see the estate up in the foothills of the Eastern Carpathian Mountains. After adjusting my bag, I trekked forward toward my surprise inheritance. Good thing I travel light.

Finally, I made my way to the front yard—if you could call it that. It was huge with lush greenery and blossoms of all sorts scattered around the whole lawn as if "Grandma" had simply never mowed and allowed the wild flowers to just grow…well…wild. It was beautiful.

The house itself was stone, covered with vines, moss, and what looked like little mushrooms engulfing the structure. It was old, but it was grand. There were iron brackets on a heavy, wooden arched door, with a knocker the size of two fists.

I knocked, though I'm not sure why. It was my house now, supposedly, but it felt rude of me to not knock. You could imagine my surprise then when someone did come to the door before I had a chance to put the key in.

"Good morning, ma'am. Might you be Brie Covell?"

"I am."

"Please, do come in. I apologize for my tardiness in leaving, but I dare say I wasn't expecting you until a bit later."

"No worries."

"In that case, I will leave you with this." The caretaker handed me a letter which held something heavier than paper in it as well. "On my way out, I'll check the perimeter and I'll be on my way."

"Okay. May I ask your name?"

"Of course. Where are my manners? I am Octavian Sala. I'll be coming by the house a few times a week…more when you need me to."

"What does that mean? More when I need you to?"

"Everything you need is in the envelope, Ms. Covell." He covered my hand with his and left out the front door.

It had been a long flight and a red-eye at that—all I wanted to do was sleep. After locking myself in, I took my bag upstairs and ventured for a room. It was easy enough to find one as the house had a count of five bedrooms on this floor alone. Without unpacking anything other than my toothbrush and phone charger, I plopped myself on a bed in the green room.

Plants decorated the room. There was a perfect reading area in the bay window which oversaw the back gardens. The bedspread was white, making the deep green pop even more. I could hardly believe I was on the other side of the world. Even though the excitement bubbled, I couldn't help but close my eyes.

By the time I woke up from my nap, the sun was setting over the garden. My stomach growled, begging me to feed it. Remembering the envelope Octavian had given me, I picked it up off the nightstand and headed back downstairs where I assumed the kitchen was.

Thankfully, the kitchen was stocked full of food—from frozen pizza to gourmet ingredients fit for any estate owner. Still recovering from the trip, I went for the easy bake. Pizza is always going to get a "yes" from me.

While the oven preheated, I set the letter on the kitchen island, and walked around the main floor. There was a library with more books than I could count, let alone read. The dining room was grand with a gold and red color scheme which went perfectly with the antique-looking wooden furniture. There were a couple empty rooms, one seemed suitable for a study, and the last room on the main level was locked.

Up on my tippy toes, I felt around for a key on the top of the door frame, but other than your typical dust, there wasn't anything there.

I heard the oven ding, signaling I could put the pizza in. After doing so, with the locked door still holding my attention, I hiked myself up onto the kitchen island and ripped open the envelope. The letter read:

> *My darling granddaughter,*
>
> *I can't begin to tell you how much I dreamt we had met. I'm sure you have questions about*

me, about your mother, maybe even about yourself. Things which were never explained to you. Things that were kept from you. I am sorry I couldn't be a part of your life then to fill in the blanks, but I had given my word to your mother that I wouldn't intervene as long as I lived. Now that I have moved on, I can open some doors for you.

Enclosed is a key. The second of thirteen, the first being the key to the house itself. All the keys belong to a room in this house, and will be presented to you in the order in which they were meant to be opened. This is a journey for us both; however, you will be tasked with puzzle after puzzle. By the end, you will be ready to be who you were meant to be.

All my love,
Madison Covell-Newman

I had no idea what any of this meant, but there was indeed a key in the envelope. It was an old skeleton key, but not a generic one. The grooves and bumps were extremely unique. Now all I wanted to do was begin the door search, but my stomach was still growling at me. I waited for the pizza to be done, but I did not wait for it to cool down. I scarfed down a couple pieces and began my quest with the locked door I had found earlier.

I certainly hoped that the rest of this adventure was going to be as easy as this first step. The key slid right into the hole and turned perfectly, revealing a completely bare room. At first, nothing seemed out of place. There was no furniture or decor. There wasn't even another door that was easily visible. However, after feeling my way around the smooth walls, I noticed a curling of the wallpaper in one of the corners of the room.

I knew I didn't want to tear apart any part of this magnificent house, but at the same time, I was on a hunt. There was no way I was going to leave that one out-of-place piece in an otherwise pristine room untouched.

Squatting down, I pinched the corner with my thumb and pointer finger and slowly pulled upwards, keeping the natural diagonal of the paper. It took a bit of scratching with the fingernails to peel it all off, but all in all, it came off as smoothly as it felt on the wall.

A whole new wall, or rather, a wall of doors, came into view. Each was numbered with a different color or pattern on the doors—all of which were also locked.

"I should have guessed it wouldn't have been as easy as I was hoping. What did I get myself into?"

The pizza from earlier hadn't quite satisfied my stomach, so I left to retrieve the rest of the pizza I had left in the kitchen then headed back into the room. I criss-crossed my legs and stared at the wall of doors while I shoved the pizza into my mouth.

"Eleven doors." But then it clicked. The first part of the puzzle. "Maybe?" Eleven doors plus the main entrance where I inherited the first key, and the key from the envelope that started this quest, "Thirteen doors. Thirteen keys. No wonder Mother hated the number."

I guzzled down the rest of the pizza then took another look around. There had to be another key somewhere. I rechecked all the doors for the third time, but all were most definitely still locked. Nothing in the ceiling seemed out of sorts and at first glance, the floor looked to be solid as well. In a frustrated tantrum, I grabbed my dirty pizza dish and headed back to the kitchen to put it in the sink.

Upon my return to the room that seemed impossible to even exist, I lay down on my stomach just outside the door frame, thinking that maybe a different point of view might help me find something that I had previously missed. And wouldn't you know it, there was a slant in the floor.

After running back to the kitchen to grab a handful of grapes, I came back to the room, threw the grapes in and watched as they all rolled to the opposing wall, diagonal from the originally found curled wallpaper. I walked over to the corner, pushed aside the collection of grapes and saw the wood had what appeared to be a missing piece—much like one of those brain teaser puzzles that require you to fidget with the many blocks in order to create a picture.

Sure enough, that's exactly what it was. I used to love these as a kid. One came every year on my birthday. I hadn't figured it out until one year I saw my mother throw a wrapped box away. Later that night I snuck out of my room and opened it. I played with it for hours in my bedroom under the blankets with a flashlight. The years following, I kept my eyes peeled for more to arrive. It was always on the stoop before sun up, and yet, oddly enough, I never saw anyone come by to drop it off. It was simply not there one moment, and there the next.

Needless to say, after years of practice, I became rather good at them. And this was no exception—a few moves here and there and the puzzle was solved. Not that there was any picture to be seen, but a floor board nearby popped up, and there was the third key.

After finding the door to match the key, the first six doors were quite easy. Simply open and there was another key, or there was a box of sorts that would once again require some puzzle brain power. However, by the time I got to door number seven, there wasn't a ledge where anything sat, just a black hole.

Now, I wouldn't call myself a wuss when it comes to creepy, but I wouldn't say that I don't have any fears either. And I'd like to think of myself as cautionary. There were only three keys left to retrieve. I couldn't very well give up now.

Sticking my arm into a dark hole in a house which was gifted to me by a relative who had apparently been banned from my life by my own mother for unknown reasons and where I just arrived had me questioning my risks here. But in the end, I was warned that I'd be tested and I'd be damned if I wouldn't rise to the occasion.

So, in my hand went. Thankfully, I felt an object dangling in the dark abyss and easily found the black painted door that the corresponding black painted key opened.

The black door wasn't like the others, however. It was practically a full-sized door positioned close to the corner where the wallpaper had been torn up. I had a feeling the easy part of this adventure was over and done with at this point. The next task was assuredly going to force me to abandon my instincts and walk into the unknown.

I was certainly not disappointed. I opened the door and walked myself in, following a very dim glow that seemed to come from nowhere, down a very narrow and fairly short hallway. At the end of which was, of course, a door.

And of course, the door was locked. At this point, I felt a little lost. I had only two keys left to find, a total of three small doors connected to a wall, and this full-sized door and no clue as to how to retrieve the next key.

I wondered if any of the keys would be reused, but the only key I had with me in the hallway was the black one—the eleventh key. Even though my gut told me it wouldn't work, I tried it anyway, only to discover that I was right.

Walking back out into the room of doors, I sat. My stare moving among the last three little doors in the wall. At first, I didn't see any correlation between the black door and any of the three doors, until I looked closer at the handles.

One of the mini doors—the lower of the three, leaving the other two at a northwest and northeast diagonal from it—had the roman numeral for eleven etched into the center of the knob. Using the black, eleventh key, I unlocked it.

There…sat another envelope, quite similar to the one in which Octavian had given me. Not only was there a key sitting inside, but there was yet another note from my grandmother which read:

My dearest granddaughter,

We all have a destiny to fulfill in this world. However, you are a lucky one as you inherited the ability to choose your own. Just as your mother did, and I did before her. For you are a daughter of the Thirteenth Moon. An ancient coven of witches dedicated to helping those who cannot help themselves.

Our powers are gifted to us if we choose them to be, as I did when I was sixteen. Your mother chose not to use her gift, which is why she sheltered you from me and why you are much older than your typical novice witch.

There are two doors left. Both hold one of your destinies. If you choose your gift, you will be transported to the coven's school, where you will learn to control your magic and eventually inherit the title of Mother Moon.

> *If you do not choose your gift, you will return*
> *back to the house as you first found it. The house*
> *is yours either way, just know that this room will*
> *no longer exist. And though you will have*
> *memories of it, there is no turning back time.*
>
> *No matter which path you take, my dear*
> *child, know that I will be by your side, watching*
> *over you as you flourish.*
>
> *Blessed Be,*
> *Mother Moon Madison*

I backed up, though it was more like catching myself from falling backwards, until I hit the wall behind me. Sliding down, with the letter in my hands, I must have reread it a dozen times over. Finally, I broke my repetitive trance and gazed at the two remaining doors. The two doors that were told to have my life locked within them.

How would I ever decide? What if I became a witch, which felt weird in my mouth to say, and I ended up not liking it? Or the other way around? I'd be cursed to live a life in which I know of my witch bloodline, yet be expected to lead a life as I always had, yearning for answers to questions about myself, my mother, my grandmother, my past....

I reread the letter one more time. There hadn't been a time limit either. Could I simply sit in this room in limbo for a week or so to think it over?

With the knowledge and the work that I had just put in combined with still recovering from a red-eye flight to a much different timezone, I felt my body and eyes getting heavy, and dozed off.

I saw two doors ahead of me—larger versions of the mini doors—though, now, both were cracked open. On the left, a brown door engraved with my last name blew open as if a gust of wind had walked through it. The wind carried me with it, showing my home. Flashes of a dying garden came into my vision. A line of people outside the estate gate sought help for illness and ailments, to which I was only able to send away without assistance.

With another gust of wind, I was standing in front of the door on the right. It was covered in moss. Vines of fruit and flowers blooming all sorts of colors. I walked in to see a group of women standing in a circle under the clearest sky I had ever seen. A woman in the center was lying down, tears streaming down the corner of her eyes only to be soaked into the earth. A bright light flashed. The woman was now standing, smiling and dancing under the moonlight.

Then a muffled voice whispered as I was taken back to view both doors once again, "You choose your path, my child. Only then, can you fulfill your destiny." A woman appeared in front of me. She brushed tears away that I hadn't even realized were forming. "You are of the moon, granddaughter. Your life is your own."

"Grandmother?"

With another flash of light, I woke up. There before me were the two doors from my dream, exactly as I had pictured them—only these were still locked. Something told me that I had the key, even though I hadn't physically found it. I reached in my pocket and there it was—a key formed of glass. Inside were two shining strings—one gold and one bronze.

It was at that moment I knew which path I wanted to take. I placed the key into the right door covered with greenery and a vibrancy of life. The key broke as I turned it, tearing my skin in the process. Even though the door opened, there was nothing but a stone wall.

Oddly enough, I didn't panic, as I knew where the thirteenth key was. I went back through the black door, down the small hallway, and reached for the knob of the final, locked door.

As the blood from my cut seeped into the grooves, the trail illuminated, filling the door with a brilliant glow. It opened and a gust of wind fought me back, but I pushed through and found myself in a grand courtyard.

A woman walked up to me. "Welcome to Moon Academy. Your grandmother mentioned you'd be joining us a bit late. Know that we are all here to guide you on your way."

A collective group of women encircled me, joining hands, and said, "Blessed Be the Mother Moon."

THE THIRTEENTH YEAR

There was something abot freshly baked bread that seemed to do more for Bethany's alertness in the morning than coffee could ever do. The smell lured her into the bakery every morning. She often wondered if it was a blessing or a curse to live in an apartment just above the best bakery in town. But her clouded thinking was often quickly resolved with her first bite of whatever scrumptious scone, roll, or slice of a cinnamon apple loaf she chose to put in her mouth..

"Good morning, Bethany. What will it be today?" Ms. Briton was the owner of the whole building, leasing the apartments above her bakery and living in the complex herself. She had to have been one of the nicest ladies Bethany had met. She felt ever so blessed to happen into Ms. Briton's bakery when she did about thirteen years ago.

"Always such a hard choice to make. What just came out of the oven?"

Ms. Briton took a quick peek into the kitchen and came back with a plump and rosie smile. "One of my personal favorites—peach coffee cake with a pecan streusel on top."

Bethany could practically feel the cake crumbling in her mouth, puckering with the sweetness of the peach and the vibrant flavor of the crunchy topping.

"Sounds perfectly heavenly. I'll take it…with a side of whatever pairing of tea you'd suggest."

"Coming right up, dear."

After the exchange of money and treats, Bethany headed to work. She was a social worker, mainly working with teenagers. It could often be a mentally tasking job, but she was determined to help as many kids as she could.

She stepped out onto the sidewalk and went to turn right, but was knocked into by a man who thought looking at his phone was more important than keeping his eyes up and watching where he was going. Her tea jostled enough to drip onto her hand, still piping hot, and her coffee cake, though protected in a container in a paper bag, looked more like a bread pudding than a coffee cake. Not that she minded; it would taste just as delicious, but it was the principle of the matter.

"Honestly, you have two eyes. You should use them more often." Bethany, though kind hearted, had learned long ago the importance of a stern exterior when living in the big city. Plus, the hot tea scalding her hand didn't quite give her the warm fuzzies to be polite. She sucked off the liquid from her skin.

"I'm terribly sorry. You're right. I should use them more. Emails can wait anyway, right? I suppose that's what an office is for."

Not meaning to, Bethany giggled at his unexpected admittance to clumsiness. As she reached out to retrieve her coffee peach crumble, she locked eyes with him. Razor blades on fire—that's what it felt like as her blood pumped harder and her heart quickened to an ungodly pace.

"Not a problem." All but snatching the bag out of his hands, she turned to leave his presence, only to be yanked back by a hand hooking her elbow.

"I said I was sorry. There's no reason to be a bitch about it."

She could feel a burning rush of tears building. Curling both lips in and biting down, she did a couple blinks and released a breath that she hadn't realized she had been holding in.

Bethany forced a smile and opened her eyes. "Of course. I'm sorry. Just been an…unexpected morning so far. I shouldn't have taken it out on you, though."

He let go of her arm.

"Would you allow me to make it up to you?"

"Now that's more like it. What did you have in mind?" He shuffled closer to her.

Keeping the forced smile plastered on her face, she took a step back. Just enough so she could breathe.

"Could I buy you a drink or two? Maybe later this evening?"

He stepped towards her again. "Your place or mine?"

A chuckling, nervous laugh escaped as she, again, took a step back.

"I was thinking about dinner first. How about 'The Rocks' bar at 'Hotel Lush' at eight o'clock?"

"I'm free right now." Finally getting the hint, he stopped inching closer to Bethany, much to her relief, though her insides shook like a category five earthquake.

"You may be free, but some people have work on Monday mornings." She tried her best to flirt and prayed that he couldn't see right through her.

"Such a pity...a creamed delight sounded good this morning. But, I will take you up on the drinks. See you tonight."

"See you there." She turned to whisk away, but his voice stopped her once again.

"Do you have a name?"

She paused. "Lynn." Bethany's middle name.

"Does that come with a last name?"

"O'Connor." She had no idea where that name came from but any name was better than her real one.

"Looking forward to it."

Bethany simply nodded with the same frozen plastic smile, then pivoted on her heels and walked as fast as she could without running. Her stomach bubbled, knowing he was watching her ass as she walked away from him. As soon as she turned the corner out of view, she vomited, no longer able to keep the acidic disgust at bay.

After thirteen years, an entire lifetime ago, the man who had broken her had returned. The man who had violently raped her had wandered back into her life with no recollection of who she was or how much damage he had caused—no care in the world other than to do it all over again.

Bethany wiped her mouth, took a swig of coffee, swirled it around in her mouth, then spat out any bile remnants. *I'd rather die than to have him uproot the life I had to rebuild because of him. But...watching him suffer...now that might be worth it.*

Though Bethany went to work, her mind was preoccupied by the events of the morning and the planning for what was to come next. After a fairly late lunch, she convinced her boss to let her go home early due to a "headache" that she just couldn't seem to shake.

Instead of going home, however, she made her way to her storage unit. She honestly didn't know why she still had it as the items inside held little to no value to her anymore, but in this very moment, she was all too glad she had it at her disposal, for what she had planned would require a secluded place.

Bethany had dreamed of her revenge against her attacker for years—not knowing that she'd actually have a chance to be vindicated, but she was confident she could pull it off. She just needed to acquire one more thing before meeting up with….

She had just realized that she didn't even know the man's name. All these years later, after gaining the courage to report the attack a few weeks after it had occurred, there had been no lead in the case, not even a mention in the papers about it.

And now, even if she could get a sample of his DNA, too much time had passed. The statute of limitations had run out. He would be able to simply walk away…again. Who knows if there were others, but if Bethany had to guess, she knew she hadn't been the only one brutalized by this man.

Bethany locked up the storage unit then headed for her car. She dialed a number on her cellphone that she had vowed never to call again—even changed the name to "Poison". But this time was different; it had to be the exception to the rule.

"Hey, Jimmy."

"Long time, Baby Beth. Looking for some fun, again?"

Bethany bit her bottom lip. Her hand shook as she held the phone up to her ear. Her armpits began to sweet, remembering the feeling of utter weightlessness. The rush of the warm, wet blanket coursing through her veins would always be a refreshing thought, but she couldn't let her past drug addiction, hiding from the trauma of the very same man she would be seeing again tonight, cloud her end game.

"I'm just looking for Liquid X."

"Aww. Some GHB. Some Cherry Meth. Some Easy Lay."

"Yes!" I blurted. I couldn't take his carefree listing of a drug that was not only used on me, but used on others, making them vulnerable to horrific ordeals.

"Easy there, Baby Beth. I'll tell you what, I'll make it worth your while. Free of charge with a purchase of your old time favorite."

She cringed her neck with her eyes closed. The thought of drifting away from the man's face once again, not a worry in the world, was tempting for the slightest moment. *I can't run this time.*

Bethany inhaled through her nose with a tightened jaw, and as she exhaled she responded through clenched teeth, "No. Just the Liquid X."

"Whatever you say, baby. See you in fifteen at the normal spot."

Without as much as a "bye", Bethany hung up. Chills crawled through her body as she tried to rid her mind of the potential high that she just passed up.

Backing up out of the storage unit's parking space, Bethany headed for the bridge.

Jimmy—"the Troll", as he was also known—had his stomping grounds under the bridge since before he became Bethany's dealer, which happened by accident…

Bethany had just been attacked and raped when her attacker got up to go to the bathroom, leaving her on a mattress in an old house that was set to be demolished the following day. She only knew this because the man had said he was part of the demolition team prior to beating her up, making it the perfect spot for the crime to occur. When he left, Bethany had finally regained some movement of her body, enough to get herself up and drop from the broken window.

She knew she was hurt enough where she couldn't run, which made her worry if the man would catch up to her. Seconds after escaping, Bethany heard the storm door of the house snap shut. Picking up her pace as best as she could, she heard his voice ring out.

"Thanks for the good time, baby. Let me know when you want round two." The hyena-like chortelling reverberated through every broken rib, matching the rhythm of the throbbing in her face. Although she tried to stop them, tears poured down her face, and even their light touch made her wince.

Not knowing exactly where she was, all she could do was wander, hoping someone would help her, and at the same time, wishing it was all over. That's when she stumbled under the bridge.

A man leaning against a pillar of the bridge lit a cigarette.

It startled Bethany, but she was desperate. "Help," she managed to whisper out as she got closer and closer to the stranger in the shadows.

It was Jimmy. He caught her just as she was collapsing. All she remembered after that were snippets between blackouts. He gave her water and some pills. She was in a car, driving with the windows down. The wind kept waking her up as she drifted in and out of consciousness. Finally, she woke up in the hospital.

After a few days, she was discharged, still broken and bruised. She had no desire to go back to her college—that's where the man had grabbed her to begin with—but standing outside the hospital, there was someone there to pick her up. The man in the shadows.

"Is there somewhere I can drop you off?"

Though Bethany had little recollection of who this man was, she somehow felt safe with him. "A house on the corner of Baby's Breath and Maple. I room with a few college students."

"I'll take you there if you want."

Not really wanting to walk all the way there, as her feet were still sore from glass she had come across on her journey from the house to the bridge, she went with him.

The ride had been fairly quiet after the normal pleasantries of exchanging names. That was why Bethany would forever be known by Jimmy as Baby Beth, given her name and the cross street she lived on. Once they arrived, Jimmy gave Bethany a paper bag.

"You'll be in pain for a lot longer than what the doctors said. Think of this as the extended refills they'll surely deny you. When you run out, I'll be under the Thirteenth Street bridge."

Bethany simply nodded her head with a painful curl of her mouth. Her left eye was still swollen and her busted lip was healing with a couple of stitches.

She braced her ribs with one arm, taking the bag with the other, then got out of the car and watched as Jimmy drove away.

Bethany's mind flashed back to the present. Having been to the spot under the bridge so many times before, she managed to get there on autopilot even through her blast-to-the-past haze.

Jimmy was smiling at her, as if the prodigal daughter had finally returned.

Bethany got out of the car, cash in hand, and walked under the bridge's shadow.

Jimmy's "bodyguards" were playing poker at a nearby makeshift table, which was once a spool of cable.

"Baby Beth…So good to see you again after all these years."

"Look, Jimmy, I don't want to play your games. Just here for the drugs."

"Aren't they all." The slimy smile of his forced Bethany to clench her teeth.

She stuck out the money, glaring at him, waiting for him to take it. He did. And in return, Jimmy handed off a paper bag, much like the many she had received from him for those eight long months of addiction, thirteen years ago.

Bethany turned on her heels.

"We have a bowl of some of your favorites…if you're feeling lucky…."

She froze. All those years ago, when she didn't quite have enough money, she was offered to play trick-or-treat. A bowl of all sorts of pills were mixed together. You'd roll a die and that was how many you'd take. "For Free," they would say. But it really meant for sex, as most of the time, whatever the concoction, it would knock you out, giving Jimmy and his henchmen the chance at sex.

"I paid for mine." She held up the bag then continued to her car.

As she drove off, she could see Jimmy waving in the rearview mirror.

"Fucking slimball."

Bethany headed for her apartment, taking the bag with her, and got ready for her "date". The mere thought of the word formed a ball of vomit in the back of her throat.

After getting ready, she inspected the bag, ensuring it was indeed what she had ordered. To her surprise, not only was the Liquid X there, but so was a baggie of her past demons. Hydrocodone, Oxy, Ativan, and Xanax.

"Motherfucker!" She threw the smaller baggie against the wall, gathered her things, and headed for the door…then she paused, closed her eyes, leaned back her head, and allowed a tear to slide towards her ear.

Bethany retrieved the baggie of prescription drugs, placed them in her purse, turned off the light, and locked her door.

Bethany promised herself she'd only have a couple shots of courage before the man showed up, which is why she found herself at the bar at seven thirty—a half an hour before her "date". She felt she needed the boost, but she didn't want to risk having a clouded mind for the upcoming events.

Eight o'clock rolled around. The man showed up, right on time.

"Lynn. You didn't stand me up." He sounded surprised and it made Bethany wonder if she was doing the right thing. Digging up the past, in this case, would give her a sense of closure, or so she thought, but she realized maybe it was just fueling a fire that was already burnt to a crisp. Maybe there was no need to resurrect it, and she had had the option to stand him up, apparently. But it was far too late for second guessing now. She was here. He was here. All Bethany could do now was to move forward.

"Of course. And we were so busy earlier sorting out the details of our date that I missed your name."

"Michael."

"Do you have a last name with that?" She raised her eyebrow, throwing his snide remark from earlier back into his face.

"Solomon—of Solomon Construction."

"Ah. Dare I say, I'm in the presence of an entrepreneur?"

"Indeed you are. Hey, I have to take a piss before we begin this lovely evening. Order me a drink, will you?"

Though it was technically a question, she knew it was more of a demand.

"Of course. Let me guess. You're a whiskey kind of guy."

"You already know me so well." He came behind her, kissing her cheek. "Getting to the end game faster than I was expecting."

He left for the bathroom.

She felt the ball of vomit return, but squashed it down with a forced smile to the bartender and ordered the drinks—one for him and one last one for her.

Truth be told, she knew whiskey was a pretty popular choice, but there was the faintest memory of the smell of whiskey pumping onto her face when he had been forcing himself onto Bethany years ago.

The bartender returned with two glasses, setting them in front of Bethany.

Michael was still in the bathroom. Now was her chance.

The bartender tended to other customers, distracting him from Bethany spilling the liquid in one of the glasses. She slid the vile back into her purse and began sipping her own drink so she could more easily distinguish which was hers and which was Michael's.

Michael returned. "Thanks for the drink." He slung it back in one gulp, then called for the bartender. "Another."

Bethany was under the assumption that Michael would have taken a little more time with the drink, but since he didn't, she had to speed up the action plan.

"You know, Michael. I'm not all that hungry. What do you say to you coming to my place for another night cap?" The thought of touching any part of this man without a blunt object in hand repulsed Bethany to no end, but she had to be convincing enough to get him to do what she wanted before the drugs kicked in.

Thankfully, he was happy to oblige. Bethany settled the bar tab and pulled Michael by the hand to her car.

By the time they rolled into the storage unit, Michael was unable to question them being there. He reminded Bethany of a zombie—completely zoned out, fading in and out, and his body was all but molded into the passenger seat.

She helped him get out of the car, opened her storage unit, and tied him to a chair that sat in the center of her little cube.

Having experienced this drug herself with the role reversed, Bethany knew that he wouldn't remember all of her speech she had prepped, but she had plenty of tools to help wake him up if he passed out at an inconvenient time.

A bat was her first weapon of choice—aiming for his shins, ensuring he wouldn't be able to run once the drugs wore off. The clank of the bat followed by the cracking of bones and moans from Michael, oddly enough, seemed to calm Bethany's nerves, fueling her adrenaline with the rage she had kept pent up for thirteen years.

With the rush, it was hard for her to stop, so before she blew it by killing him too fast, she dropped the bat. She began her speech.

"Michael. I think, if you look down deep into your soul, if you have one, you'll remember me. Let me tell you a story. I was newly twenty-one and studying at the university. Just the basic subjects as I still had no idea what I wanted to be when I grew up. I had changed my focus about four times since I first started. Anyway, I remember being in the library, studying, as most do in such a place. You came over to me. You were polite..much more so than you were this morning. Sure you had your cheesy pickup lines, but that was part of your charm..like you almost knew they were cheesy and yet you insisted on using them anyway."

Michael began to slump in the chair and dangled his head.

Bethany grabbed an "X-Acto" knife, slicing upwards from the corner of his nose, just missing his eye, and into his hairline.

He huffed awake with a half-hearted whine.

"Stay with me, Michael. It's rude to fall asleep in the middle of a conversation. I'll speed it up, shall I? You took me to the sports bar just off of campus. We stayed and enjoyed a few drinks. I said I was ready to go home once it got late enough. I had a test the next day, you know. I went to the bathroom, only to return with another round for us both. 'One more drink. For me. Then I'll gladly take you home.' you said with such a charming smile. I couldn't say 'no'. So I stayed. I drank. I remember you dragging me out of the bar and placing me into a truck. Next thing I knew…"

Michael was dozing again. This time, Bethany took the "X-Acto" knife and plunged it into his groin, not knowing exactly what she sliced, but he woke up as blood was inking his pants.

"As I was saying…next thing I knew, I was on something soft in a house with a broken window. You were blabbering about demolishing the building the next day. Then I saw the toes of your boot heading for my face. My head was pounding and the room spun. I closed my eyes, only to feel more kicking on my ribs, stomach, and more on my face."

Bethany tried as she might to hold back tears, but the flood gates were open. She controlled her voice, ensuring she didn't crack or squeak.

"I must have passed out because when I came to again, you were in me. It hurt. I passed out again. Finally, I opened my eyes. My head was still pounding, but the room no longer spun, and I saw you walk into the other room. I bit my cheeks so that I wouldn't moan as I got myself up and threw myself over the window. I heard your voice chase after me…and the laughter."

Bethany wiped her face. Michael had passed out. She didn't know at what point in her speech he had done so, but it didn't matter anymore. She said her peace. There was nothing more to say.

She thrusted the "X-Acto" knife into his groin again, leaving it there. Michael was only capable of gasping a moan before lights out.

Bethany locked up her storage unit, throwing the key in a ditch next to where she had parked in the parking lot and headed home, but she didn't go in right away—rather, she zoned out in the car, tears still trailing down her face as she slowed her breathing, hoping to stop her heart from feeling as though it was about to burst from her chest.

Then she remembered the bag Jimmy had given her. The one she threw against the wall…the one she retrieved…the one that sat in her glove box at this very moment.

Unlatching the compartment, she could see the little baggie peeking out. She admired the colors of the pills. Bethany grabbed them, ran past the smell of the sweet bakery, and locked herself in her apartment.

After tossing her keys and purse to the side, she sat on her couch and stared at the pills. Visions of her own attack and the images she created from the events at the storage unit now consumed her. Once again she admired the colors of Jimmy's gift.

"Oh, how beautiful you look, my old friends."

THE THIRTEENTH SEAL

It was a Monday morning, but not your typical one. Many Mondays I remember loathing and simply wishing I could stay in bed, but today had to be different. I was assigned a new precinct and was fully prepared to start it off on the right foot.

A new adventure awaited me. Lead detective had always been the goal—I just hadn't expected to be back in Chicago, my hometown—if you can count an orphanage as home. Not only was this my first time back in the city after many years of doing my best to stay away, but I was joining the task force in the middle of a publicly heated case.

I glanced in the mirror in a small entryway to my apartment. Although I told myself to be confident, the birthmark stretching from the bridge of my nose, barely missing my eye, and ending in the middle of my cheek often created wavering doubts. However, I swore I would no longer see the mark as a weakness.

"Kimberly Welsh. Get your shit together." I huffed at my reflection, putting it in its place, and marched out the door.

It was a nice couple of blocks of walking. The department supplied me with a car, but I kept it parked at the precinct. At about seven thirty in the morning, the streets were already bustling with people scurrying to their jobs, completely unaware of each other and what the day truly had in store for them. Watching people and trying to sort out their story was my favorite hobby. Most, I suppose, call that "judging", but I like to look at it as "assessing". I found it an extremely important talent to be able to tell if someone was lying or pretending to be someone they're not—uncovering secrets they try to hide behind with masked faces and closed doors.

When the elevator doors opened to the third floor I was surprised to see panic in my new team. I made my way through them, nudging and pushing when needed, and found the very person I needed, "Detective Donaldson!"

"Detective Welsh, call me Reggie. You are my replacement afterall."

"Fine. Reggie, what is all the chaos about?"

"'The Notary' has struck again."

Sure the name wasn't one to strike fear into the public like "The Ripper" or "The Night Stalker", but "The Notary" was fitting given how he marked his victims.

"He doesn't seem to waste much time."

"You're telling me. Have you been briefed yet?"

"I read some of the file that you emailed to me, but it doesn't seem detailed enough to go on."

"That's because this guy isn't giving us much—until now, that is." Reggie grinned, a small, tired grin, but a grin nonetheless. He had put in his notice to retire at either the end of this case or at the end of the month, whichever came first. And I can't say that I blame him. He had given many years to the force. I think he found this case as his swan song, if you will, and after all, this was day eleven of "The Notary's" rapes and killings.

"I'll brief you on the way to the crime scene."

Having yet to settle into my desk and new office, I followed Reggie back down the elevator and to his car, which would soon be mine.

"This is the closest he has been to the city." He tossed me a map with red circles on it. They were almost in a perfect line with the names of each victim assigned a circle. "The killings started in Twines, a small town housing only a couple hundred people, most of whom are the fine educators and students of Atticus Academy, the All Boys Rehabilitation and Refinery School between Spring Grove and Antioch. After breaking through some red tape with the school's privacy policy, they told us a kid had escaped the night before the graduation ceremony. The suspect is Andrew Lowan. His parents sent him to Atticus Academy when he was fourteen. He was set to graduate with a focus in journaling and creative writing."

"Has anyone made contact with the parents yet?"

"No. After we take a look at the most recent victim, you and I will head that way."

When we arrived at the scene, you could smell the blood in the air with notes of burnt flesh. The sight of the woman brought vomit into my throat. This wasn't my first dead body to come across, but the manner in which it was displayed and desecrated was unlike anything I'd ever seen.

The victim's underwear had been shoved into her mouth, which the killer had done to about half of the girls. My guess was they attempted to scream and fight back. Her clothes were folded neatly and left beside her body which was positioned like a hog on a spick with an apple in its mouth. Her hands were tied above her head with her hair draping down over her face.

There was no visible sign of the wax seal which he had used previously as a signature of his work, though I had a feeling it would be discovered on the other side of her body. And sure enough, after pictures were taken and the body was prepped to be taken to the morgue, the circular waxed seal had been put on display on her forehead—strands of hair intertwined with the now cold, hardened wax.

Seeing pictures of the other victims was bad enough, but seeing it in person, mixed with the smell of burning flesh and death, and the visual of what this monster had done to her took me to a whole other state of revulsion.

"Incredible, isn't it?" A C.S.I. employee murmured, probably louder than he had intended as he cleared his throat after locking eyes with me. I noticed his slight smirk and the appearance of an ounce of almost admiration in his voice, which nearly equally disgusted me. "I only mean that it's incredible how different people think. What could have happened in this person's life to imagine something so sick and twisted?" He blinked a couple times, waiting to see if my facial features would soften at his explanation, but when I continued to stare, he looked away and continued his job without another word.

"Welsh!" Reggie had called. "You ready to head to the Lowan residence?"

"Yes, Sir." I made my way back to the car and buckled up.

We pulled away from the crime scene. I found it odd that looking out the window, which normally sparked joy as it fueled my "people-watching" habit, had dulled—as if the world now had a gloomy, gray cloud hovering over it, making me question life itself. I just wasn't sure if it was because of the crime scene or if it was due to the C.S.I's curious comment.

"This is only the beginning, Welsh. If you want to back out, now would be your time."

"No. I'm fine. Just a different perspective than what I was expecting. I wasn't expecting…"

"The pictures never do the scene justice."

"No. They don't." Though I wasn't looking at Reggie, I could feel his gaze on me. "Was there something else?"

"I don't know what you and the crime scene investigator were discussing, but I suggest not taking what they say to heart. It's bad enough that we see the big picture. They see all the little details. Have their hands on it. That's gotta do something to the mind."

"Yeah. I imagine it would."

The rest of the drive was quiet, not in an awkwardly silent sort of way, just introspectively numb in thought. Reggie got out of the car first, slamming his door behind him. I took a deep breath then followed behind him up the stairs to the front porch of the Lowan house.

Mr. Lowan answered the door and invited us both in.

"We were wondering how long it was going to take for you to arrive."

"If that's the case, why didn't you reach out to us sooner?" I asked. Reggie shot me a look, and yet still, I waited for Mr. Lowan to answer. He was a tall, thin man with boldly rimmed glasses. He had dark hair, which you could see was dyed, and bushy eyebrows to match.

Mrs. Lowan appeared delicate, both in her mannerisms of offering tea with a shaky hand and physically. Her skin had an ashy tone to it. Her eyes and cheek bones were slightly sunken, and her hair was speckled with whites and grays.

Mrs. Lowan answered, "We were told by the school and their lawyer to keep quiet until you came to us."

"Don't you think that points negatively at your son?"

"Would it have changed anything?" Mrs. Lowan looked directly at me, her stare unwavering. There was a stern hollowness in her voice and expression.

"You know he's behind these murders, don't you?"

"Yes."

"Lorraine."

She shot her husband a look.

"He's our son."

"Yes. And he is not a good boy, Roger."

While Roger grumbled under his breath and walked into the kitchen, Lorraine sat on the couch and motioned for Reggie and me to sit on the two chairs across from her. She waited patiently until we were settled with our cups of tea, took a sip for herself and began.

"Andrew had always been an odd child. His early years involved trapping and keeping all sorts of insects in his room. One day I walked in to pick up his laundry and he was dissecting a beetle of sorts."

Reggie joked, "Practicing for a morgue career."

"It was still alive," she responded quite matter of factly with no change in her expression.

Reggie sank into his chair a bit.

"As he got older there were incidents around the neighborhood. Our neighbor Margret's cat disappeared. He was an indoor cat and the woman hardly left her home. Not much of a life if you ask me, but about a week after the cat vanished, Andrew did too. We couldn't find him anywhere until he just appeared back in his bedroom one morning.

We never could get him to tell us where he had been or what he had been doing."

"Is that why you sent him off to Atticus Academy?"

"Yes…and no."

"What do you mean?"

"We have a daughter, Denise. Roger and I had her at a fairly young age. It was her first year of college when she returned for winter break to visit. Andrew was thirteen at the time, just about to be fourteen. Roger and I never really went out by ourselves, afraid of what we might come home to with Andrew by himself, but since Denise was in town, we asked her to stay at the house with him while we went on a much needed date night."

"I checked in about every half hour, which Roger will tell you defeats the purpose and mood of a date night…"

"It does!" He yelled from the kitchen.

She rolled her eyes, but continued as if nothing had been said. "Denise's reports were reassuring, until the last one."

"What happened?"

"The check for dinner was on its way. I decided to call one more time before we headed home. Denise took longer to answer, almost letting the phone go to the answering machine. And when she did answer, her voice was shaky and she was breathing heavily. I asked if she was okay. She said that she was but I knew different. Right after we paid, we rushed home. Denise was sitting on the couch, tears streaming down her face, but her pointer finger was on her lips. We rounded the couch corner to find Andrew's head laying in her lap."

"That's not too odd for a brother and sister, is it?" Reggie leaned forward, furrowing his brows. He looked lost and impatient.

"I suppose alone, it wouldn't be too out of the ordinary. Roger woke Andrew up and sent him off to bed while I talked to my daughter once she was finally able to talk through the tears. Andrew had come onto her…" Lorraine lowered her voice. This was the first time since we started talking that Lorraine had come across as embarrassed. "...groping at her breasts and reaching down. She pushed him away before his fingers could go in, but that only made him more determined. Denise said he cornered her in the kitchen, grabbing at her clothes trying to rip them off."

"How did she manage to get away?"

"My phone call saved her. The phone rang. Denise managed to convince Andrew that if she didn't answer, we'd know something was wrong and come home right away, only to disturb them in their moment alone. He let her pass and answer the phone. Not that she knew it at the time, but she told him that we were on the way home, so now wouldn't be a good time for them to be together." Lorraine raised her hand to her nose as if stifling her disgust. "He fell asleep on her lap, and that's how we found them. After that night, Roger and I knew we had to do something."

"So there you have it. We sent our son away, to save our girl, and now he's coming back for what he really wants." Roger was standing in the shadows of the living room, just outside the kitchen.

"Denise." I realized after blurting it out loud that it was in poor taste, but I couldn't take it back now. Lorraine wiped her face before tears could touch her cheek. Roger simply nodded, knowing it was the truth.

"You think he's making his way back home for Denise?" Reggie understood the motive but I could tell a question was still weighing on his chest. "Why kill so many before reaching his target?"

"It's a game." I noticed a family photo on the mantel. I stood up and lifted it closer.

"That was our last family picture. Right before we sent him away."

"The victims as a whole may not seem to have a connection, but Reggie, a part of each victim, the part that he…" I looked at the poor mother's eyes. I couldn't bring myself to say it in front of her. Even though she knew in her heart that her son was a monster, it was still her child. "I'm sorry. But may I take this picture with me for now?"

"Of course. Anything you need." Lorraine cleared her throat, willing herself not to break down. Roger joined her at her side, laying his hand on her shoulder.

"Before we leave, I have another question. Where is Denise now?"

"After college, she moved to Colorado. However, we bought her tickets to come out for a visit."

"When is she due to arrive?"

"Tomorrow evening."

I just nodded. "Thank you for your time. We'll show ourselves out."

Nudging Reggie towards the door, I saw Lorraine stand and embrace her husband, finally breaking the damn of tears.

Once we were back in the car, Reggie asked, "What was all that about? You were in the middle of, what I thought, was a lightbulb moment, but then you cut yourself off."

"Not only have they dealt with a daughter who was sexually assaulted by their son, but now their son is the prime suspect in eleven rapes and murders and counting. They didn't need to hear my lightbulb moment."

"You're one of those empathetic detectives." He chuckled. "See how long that gets ya."

I scowled at him, but shared my new insight. "As I was saying in the house, not one of the victims looks like Denise as a whole. But break down their features…" I rummaged through my file bag and pulled out the pictures of the victims. "Something about each victim resembles Denise. The very body part in which he has marked with his wax seal. I bet you if we take those parts and put them in a photoshop program, the end result would look like Denise's twin."

Reggie grabbed the pictures of each victim before they had been disgraced and puzzle-pieced them together. Sure enough, it closely resembled Denise in the Lowan's last family picture.

"Given this so-called map we now have, the only missing part is her lips. What do you suppose he'll go after once the picture is finished?"

"Lips tomorrow, then Denise will be home. He won't have to fantasize anymore. He'll have the real thing."

"Unless we stop him." Reggie put the car in gear after throwing my files onto my lap and backed out of the Lowen's driveway. "Let's head back to the office. See if we can figure out where he'll be next."

"How, with our department-regulated fortune teller's ball?" I snickered at my own joke.

"No." Popping my bubble instantly. "We have a task force digging into patterns of the events. I think it's time we offer them a fresh look on things."

Rather than putting the files back, I used the time to comb through each one again, hoping that something would click and we could prevent any more deaths. And by the time we got back to the precinct, I wanted nothing more than to put the files aside. The pictures and details of the crime had given me a migraine I felt would never resolve. They would somehow always be a part of me.

I walked into the building very differently than I had that morning—looking down at the floor with what I'd imagined were the last thoughts of the victims swimming around in my mind, instead of the excitement of the new job charged with glowing eagerness. I followed Reggie into a conference room. A total of one officer made up the task force.

"So by task force you mean—"

He interrupted me as we walked in the door. "He, alone, is worth the title 'task force'. Liam Baker is a fantastic detective—extremely detail oriented and the only one I'd trust to find any kind of sense in this chaos."

I held up my hands in surrender. "Understood."

A corkboard was cluttered with pins, pictures, a map, and a few strings in the middle of a bunch of desks circling it. The man I presumed was Liam Baker stood in the center staring at the board. His dark hair was in shambles, he had a string of coffee cups lining the tables, and his necktie was loosened with the top couple buttons of his shirt popped and no longer tucked into his pants—a scene I could only expect of a detective who wouldn't quit until the killer was found. How long had this guy been up?

"Liam, this is Detective Kimberly Welsh, my replacement. Kimberly, this is Detective Liam Baker."

Liam barely acknowledged me with a wave of his fingers while still making eye contact with the board before him. Not that I could blame him. These were horrific murders. I wanted nothing more than to see Andrew Lowan behind bars, but Reggie tapped on his shoulder, anyway.

Liam turned. His eyes sunken with purple bags and a five o'clock shadow on what I presumed was normally a clean-shaven face—a handsome devil. The glinting of his blueish-green eyes drew me in like the hypnotic movement of the ocean's tide.

"My apologies." His voice was deeper than expected and on the raspy side.

I felt the heat crawl to my cheeks. *You're in the middle of an investigation, Kimberly. Stop it.*

"Not at all. I completely understand. We actually came to help and feed you with more information."

"Feed me, huh?" A small crick in his lips curled up into a tired, yet playful, smile. "I haven't eaten since…" he glanced at his watch, "Oh. I suppose it was dinner last night."

Sure enough, I turned to see the Chinese boxes sitting there, lid open and chopsticks poking out.

"Any places deliver?" I had to be honest, my stomach was growling too.

"'Mad Pies' is just across the street. Pizza will be here in no time. James!" Reggie shouted out of the room. A young, baby-faced officer ran up to attention. Reggie told him to order a few pies and bring them back.

While we waited, Reggie and I filled Liam in on the information we had learned from the suspect's parents.

"That's one mystery solved—knowing who we are looking for—but how can we predict where he'll hit next?"

James returned with piping hot pizza. Liam wasted no time and shoved a piece in his face.

With pizza in hand, I stared at the cork board, then asked, "These tacks represent the locations of the victims, right?" There were eleven in a slightly scattered line. The last of which was the location in which Reggie and I had visited just a few hours ago. "Not only are they making their way to the Lowan's front door, they seem almost evenly spaced. About every five miles and keeping fairly close to the highway. Am I wrong?"

Liam grabbed another piece of pizza then stood by me, analyzing my possible findings. "I think you're right.

And if that's the case," Liam put his pizza down on a desk, picked up a tack and a marker, then stabbed the board and made a perimeter. "Then Andrew will strike again around here. In our neck of the woods."

"I'll be damned if he gets another one." Reggie was sitting on the desk, his arms crossed. "Looks like it'll be another long night. You guys up for a stake out?" I suppose Reggie knew that Liam would be down, as he looked directly at me when asking the question.

"Yes, sir."

He glared at me.

"Reggie. Yes I am, Reggie."

He tossed me the keys. "Go home and change. Liam and I will gather a few more recruits and wait for you to return, then we'll head out."

"Why do I have to change?"

"Because you look like a cop—black pants, buttoned up, blue-collared shirt, and your hair is tied back into a bun. Go home and change."

Liam huffed out a laugh.

I walked out the door and hurried to the car. This was my chance to prove I could be an asset to the force. I knew it wouldn't take me long as I lived just down the street, but I still hurried up to my apartment, changed, and scurried back to the office.

Reggie, Liam, and a few other men and women were standing around in everyday clothes. After switching from a marked to an unmarked car, the three of us stayed in one vehicle and headed to the center of our stake out. Other units were placed at other locations surrounding us.

After getting our earpieces situated, Reggie put Liam and me together sitting on a bench as a couple, while he leaned against a newspaper stand across the street. We were in a fairly highly populated community with apartment buildings and some houses all around us.

At first there wasn't much conversation. Just three people loitering on the Chicago streets at night, but the silence was beginning to make me feel tired, so, I struck up a conversation.

I glanced down at Liam's hand where he wore a ring on his married finger. "Are you married?"

Still casually looking around, Liam gulped before answering, "No."

"Oh. I get it. Making sure your cover isn't broken. I should have thought of that…putting a ring on that finger."

"It isn't that either." He was looking right at me now. His still tired features became more tense. "I was married." Liam glanced over to where Reggie was, who happened to be looking in their direction, as he too could hear their conversation. "Reggie's daughter, Laura, and I had been married for three years."

"Oh my God, I'm so sorry. I shouldn't have pressed."

"It's fine. Laura was a teacher. A couple years ago, she was in her classroom and a student of hers from home room opened fire. Only a couple of kids from her class survived. Technically, she did too. But she was never the same after that. She killed herself a couple weeks after, once all the kids' funerals were done."

I literally couldn't bite my own tongue hard enough. What a can of worms I just opened up, not only for Liam but for his father-in-law. And I still had a long night ahead of me. No amount of beating myself up would ever be able to fix that event. But when I did open my damn mouth to vomit apologies upon them both, Liam grabbed my face and kissed me.

Absolutely, not the reaction I was expecting after such a vulnerable confession, but then it hit me. We are on a stake out.

He backed off only the slightest of space between us so he could whisper. "Reggie, you have a figure inching closer to you—your three o'clock and our twelve—looks to be wearing a blazer jacket like the uniform at the school."

"Ten four. I've got eyes."

I could feel my heart racing. Not only did we have eyes on the suspect, but I had to come off of cloud nine from that kiss and shake off the guilt and embarrassment from the conversation leading up to it.

"We are close to the bus stop, so us standing when no bus is here might break our cover."

I pulled away with a smile on my face, acting the part of a loving wife. I turned my body to face the street instead of facing Liam, so that my range was wider. I could see Reggie tapping his toes. He was anxious. I could tell he wanted this file closed up and tucked away so that he could retire on top. I just hoped he had the patience to do this right.

Liam must have noticed it too. "Reggie. Don't jump the gun. Let's just see where he is going. We aren't even sure if it's him or not."

"One way to find out."

"No. Don't!"

Reggie stood up and yelled, "Andrew Lowen!"

The guy peeled himself away from the shadowy nooks of the streets. His jacket was covered in blood and was shredded, no doubt from all the previous murders. His smile was wide and pale, but true and sinister. He threw something in the air towards Reggie then bolted.

Liam and I ran across the street after Andrew, passing Reggie who had taken cover behind the newspaper stand.

Smoke emanated from the object Andrew had thrown, but before we continued to run, we got confirmation from Reggie that he was alright and for us to keep going.

We barely missed the smoke but caught sight of the tail of Andrew's uniform coat around the corner of the next block. We followed, thinking we were gaining, but when we rounded the corner, he was gone—vanished into thin air. After a solid minute or two, Liam and I headed back to the original location.

A grumbled "Ahh," and clashing of metal on pavement echoed through the buildings.

"Reggie!" I looked at Liam and we both ran.

But it was too late. Reggie was on the ground with a knife sticking out of his chest. Liam called for backup and an ambulance while I did my best to not disturb the scene yet still attend to Reggie.

"Reggie." I saw all the blood leaking from his body. I knew the ambulance wouldn't make it in time. "Reggie, I'm so sorry."

He coughed, raising his hand for Liam.

Liam hung up the phone and made his way to Reggie's side, holding his hand. "I know, Reggie. I know. Say 'hi' to Laura for me, will you?" A tear slid down his cheek.

Reggie's breaths became more and more gargled. As soon as we heard the sirens, Reggie took his last breath.

Liam placed his hand on Reggie's chest, then reluctantly backed away with me by his side. We waited for the ambulance and police to come to the scene and process it, giving our statements and waiting for the C.S.Is to process the scene, including the one I had halfway met earlier that day…or, I suppose it was yesterday at this point. When all was said and done, Liam and I left in the car, one person short of when we had arrived.

The car ride back to the precinct was quiet—a silence that hurt. The only thing we had established was the fact that going home at this juncture was futile. We had let Andrew escape. The only questions now were, who is his last victim before he goes after Denise, where is said victim, and how do we save Denise?

A mob of police and passersby crowded the station's entry. Liam pulled the car up as close as he could and we pushed our way through the crowd only to see a young woman, arms tied behind her back, in the same position as all the others, with a wax seal burnt onto her lips.

That mother fucker hit home.

Ironically, other than killing a male, everything stayed in line with Andrew's plan as even the precinct had been marked within his possible attack radius. I guess I just wasn't thinking he would be stupid enough to drop her on our front doorsteps. Though, given how last night was, I guess it wasn't such a stupid move at all—more of an in-your-face boasting move…as if saying "catch me if you can".

Liam and I made our way inside while another team worked on processing the scene outside. It was all hands on deck now. It was now day twelve, and other than Reggie, we had his last victim before Denise.

"We need to be the ones to pick Denise up from the airport. It is the only way we can protect her."

"I agree. Did the Lowens give you and…Did you get a time of arrival for Denise yesterday while speaking with the parents?"

"No…only that it was this evening."

"Let's call them and figure out the time so we are prepared."

I reached for the phone but it rang before I was able to pick it up. "This is Detective Kimberly Welsh."

"Detective. It's Lorraine."

"I was just getting ready to call you. Everything okay?"

"No. I don't believe so."

I waved my hand in front of Liam's face to get his attention. He stood up and put his ear next to the phone.

"What's wrong?"

"We tried calling Denise this morning, hoping we could convince her to stay in Colorado until we find Andrew, but she hasn't returned our calls since last night. I know it could be anything, but Detective Welsh, she always picks up the phone." Her voice was cracking and after what Lorraine had told me yesterday about how her phone call had saved her once, I whole-heartedly believed her.

"Mrs. Lowen, we will call the airlines and see if we can find something out. What airport would she have left from?"

"Denver is what the tickets were for. It's the closest."

"I'll keep you posted." I hung up only to call the O'Hare airport. Then I told Liam, "Call down to the Denver airport, see if maybe she got onto an earlier flight."

"On it."

We made our calls. All I found out was there weren't any passengers set to fly into Chicago with Denise's name or description later that evening, and before I could ask about an earlier flight, Liam called me over to his desk. I hung up my phone and I put my ear up to his phone.

"There was a change in Denise Lowen's ticket from an evening arrival for today to a 5:35 flight out this morning. It would have landed just a few minutes ago at O'Hare." Liam hung up the phone and we both darted for the doors, passing the crime scene and the crowd behind the caution tape. We raced, sirens blaring, for the airport.

Despite our call ahead to the O'Hare airport, asking for them to shut the airport down, we missed him again.

The plane had docked, passengers disembarked, and bags picked up…all but Denise Lowen's.

"Andrew must have changed her tickets."

"And picked her up."

"More like kidnapped her. She wouldn't leave for a friendly visit with him and certainly not without her bags."

"You think he'd take her home? Finish the deed there?"

I shook my head. "No. Especially since he knows we are onto him. Let's check the cameras. Look for how they left the airport. Maybe we can get a hit off a license plate."

In the security hub of the airport, we saw Andrew, arms linked, with Denise. He had something held to her back for persuasion, but we couldn't figure out what it was. Once in the parking garage, they entered a black van. There was no license plate attached to the vehicle; however, there was a piece of paper dropped in the parking lot before the vehicle exited.

We headed to the parking lot. Even though we knew we were in the right spot, we didn't see any note. We knew the chances of it still being here was slim to none, but we were rooting for the slim side of things. Liam and I had planned to talk with the parents again to see if they had any insight of where Andrew would be going. As we were heading for the elevator, a voice said, "Excuse me?"

It was a young woman whose car was across and down a few from where Andrew and Denise were.

"Do you have any change?"

"No. We don't."

"Are you sure?" She pulled out a crumpled piece of paper and held it in front of her face. "A lady dropped it just a few moments ago. Are you sure you don't have any spare change?"

Liam reached in his pocket and threw a twenty at her. "We don't have time for this. Hand it over."

She handed it to Liam.

I asked, "Why did you pick it up?"

"Well, I was sitting over there in the corner—one of the best places to find spare change. I saw the woman drop it. But when I went after them to try to give it back, the woman had tears in her eyes and the man was holding a knife. I waited for them to leave then picked it up. Then I saw you guys and wondered if you were looking for it."

"It is. Thank you for your help."

"Of course." She held out her hand, asking for more money.

"Lady, beat it before I call airport security."

She stuck her tongue out at Liam but marched away in her tube top, jean skirt, and heels that I would most definitely break something in.

Liam and I glanced at each other, a shrug and a raised eyebrow on both ends seemed to be implied, but there was no time to waste. I opened the note. It was hard to read, as she probably was only able to write it from her pocket. I got a pen out and retraced her scratches. Finally, we came to the conclusion that the paper said "Siren".

Neither of us knew what that meant, but we called Lorraine Lowen back to update and ask if the word "Siren" had any meaning to the kids.

"Yes. It's the name of our boat. We haven't been out on it in a couple of years, but we always have it ready in case Denise visits and wants to take it out."

"Where is it right now?"

"It's docked at Belmont Harbor. H dock."

"We're on our way there now." I hung up the phone again. I turned on the sirens and called down to the docks to ask for their assistance—not to get involved, necessarily, but to postpone departure if possible.

Once we pulled up to the parking lot, we noticed a gathering down on the docks. Boat security was in the water, blocking the exit to the open waters. Workers of the dock were on the docks, shouting. Then there was a scream.

We rushed down to the boat. More screams came from the cabin of the "Siren". Liam boarded first, and I followed swiftly behind him. We got on either side of the door and on the count of three, Liam busted through.

Andrew's pants were around his ankles. Denise was on her knees, arms tied behind her back with her ass in the air.

At first, I thought Denise was bleeding. Then Andrew turned around with a proud smile and a calmness in his face indicating he had succeeded in his venture. The seal stamp was in his hand.

I looked back at Denise. She wasn't bleeding, or at least not as much from what I could tell. It was red wax. Hot wax was still dripping from her freshly sealed vagina along with the remanates of Andrew's unwanted offering. Her panties soaked up her tears, as he had stuffed them in her mouth.

We were too late. Too late to save her from the trauma as a whole. As much as I was glad to have saved her life, I couldn't help but wonder if letting him finish her off would have been more beneficial—more merciful—just to save her from the turmoil and anguish she'd have to endure through the healing process ahead, both physically and mentally.

Andrew willingly dropped the seal stamp and dropped to his knees. Liam rushed over, kicking him down on his stomach to cuff him.

I tenderly made my way to Denise. I couldn't do much as moving her too much would only cause more pain and damage. But I removed her panties and unbound her, then took a blanket and wrapped her in it, positioning her curled up on her side until the medics arrived.

Liam was all too happy to bring Andrew in and begin his booking process. I stayed with Denise in the ambulance and waited until Mr. and Mrs. Lowen arrived.

Not that I wanted to, but I headed back to the office and filled out my reports while it was "fresh in my mind" though I don't believe I'll ever forget the past couple days. Certainly not what I was expecting for my first case, nor was I expecting to attend the funeral of a fellow officer in my first week.

I had only worked a few days with Reggie, and yet I felt as though we had been partners forever. I couldn't even imagine how Liam felt—the loss of his wife and now his father-in-law, and both in such violent and unnecessary ways.

After the worst first week of work of my life, I needed to decompress. My favorite way of doing so is to go to storage unit auctions. You never know what you'll find….

About the Author

Callie Rae Sutton is a short story author who has been published in three previous *"Of Words"* anthologies published by Scout Media. She is a wife and a teacher to both her preschool students and her superb daughter.

Fantasy, mythology, and crime tend to be her choices of poisons, however, Callie also dabbles in adventure and love stories with a twist.

Be sure to visit her at: TikTok @cr13sutton